**As hot water flowed over her,
easing the sore muscles in her shoulders and neck,
Stacy felt wonderful again.**

It was going to be a glorious weekend after all. She'd see to it. Reaching out, she grabbed the fluffy brown towel and stepped from the stall. Her hair was sparkling with drops of water and her skin had turned a rosy pink. Suddenly she glanced in the mirror and froze. Wayne was staring at her, a wicked grin on his face.

"What are you doing in here?" she gasped, clutching the towel more tightly around her.

"Looking for you," he said casually, leaning against the door frame.

"Well . . . now you've found me, so get out and let me get dressed."

"Sure you don't want me to stay and rub your back dry?" he suggested with a roguish gleam in his eye.

"I've done pretty well all these years without any help, thank you," Stacy answered smoothly.

Wayne smiled. "Let me show you what you've been missing, then. . . ."

Shadow on the Hill

Alexandra Kirk

GOLDEN APPLE PUBLISHERS

SHADOW ON THE HILL

A Golden Apple Publication / June 1985

Golden Apple is a trademark of Golden Apple Publishers

All rights reserved.

Copyright © 1984 by Alexandra Kirk.
Cover photograph by Photofile.
This book may not be reproduced in whole or in part, by
mimeograph or any other means, without permission.
For information address: Golden Apple Publishers,
666 Fifth Avenue, New York, New York 10103.

ISBN 0-553-19775-4

PRINTED IN THE UNITED STATES OF AMERICA

O   0 9 8 7 6 5 4 3 2 1

One

Stacy sat across the desk from her boss, Pete Arnold, her hands clenched tightly in her lap. She was fighting to contain her anger, but without much success. Her Irish temper, inherited from her mother's side of the family, was about to explode.

As Pete's voice droned on about her next assignment, she held fast to a single thought and kept repeating it: She could not do this story. No matter what her refusal might mean for her career, she simply couldn't do it. What on earth was Pete thinking about to even suggest it? Surely he could see how impossible it was. Finally, she could no longer remain silent about her objections. Her cheeks flushed a rosy pink and her short, black curls quivered with each word, as she snapped, "Are you out of your mind?"

Obviously startled by the vehemence of her outburst, Pete stared at her in confusion. It was the last reaction he'd expected. Stacy had always been so calm, professional, eager to please. She had never displayed the sort of egotistical temperament so characteristic of many well-established reporters.

He'd grown particularly fond of Stacy, when she'd served her internship here during college. She was bright and shrewd. She'd make a damn fine reporter someday, one of the best.

"Stacy, what is it? What's wrong?" he asked patiently. "I thought you would be pleased. You've been waiting for a break like this. You've been back here only a few weeks and already you're getting a chance to produce your own documentary. My God, woman, do you realize how lucky you are?"

"Pete, this has nothing to do with luck and you know it. You're exploiting my background. That would be fine, I suppose, if it weren't such an obvious conflict of interest."

Disbelief spread across Pete's face. "Conflict of interest?" he repeated, genuinely puzzled. "Stacy, that's absurd."

"Is it really?" she asked, her voice filled with sarcasm. "Pete, I campaigned for Wayne Dodge's opponent, remember?"

When he would have interrupted her, she held up her hand. "No, wait. Not only did I campaign for him, I handled all of his public relations. A lot of people know that. Do you think they would take anything I wrote about Dodge seriously? I don't see how you can expect me to do an objective documentary about him."

Pete's expression of disbelief slowly evolved into one of anger. When he spoke, it was with a cutting forcefulness.

"I expect you to do it because you are a fine journalist. I know that you won't allow whatever campaign rhetoric you spread about Dodge to influence the report you do now. Quite the contrary, in fact. I think you'll bend over backward to be fair and impartial. And," he added with emphasis, "you're right that I am exploiting your knowledge of the

2

Congressman. I assume you know more about him than anyone else on my staff. You'll do a better, more thorough job and you'll do it quickly. We need to get this on the air."

Stacy sank back in her chair and let out a sigh of defeat.

"Isn't there some way I can change your mind about this?" she pleaded.

"No," Pete said with determination, his gaze steady.

From her months as an intern at this Washington television station, Stacy knew that look. There was no way Pete would rescind his decision now.

"Okay, Pete," she said softly, "you'll get your documentary."

On her way home from the station, Stacy thought about the assignment. Pete was right about one thing: Dodge would make an excellent subject. An attractive man and a dynamic speaker, he came from a wealthy, Southern California family. The rumor back there had been that his family bought his congressional seat by outspending his opponents for television time. It was true that his campaign committee had spent a fortune, but in this last race Stacy's candidate, J.J. Lawrence, had spent every bit as much in his bid to unseat the incumbent. He'd matched Dodge commercial for commercial and both had used the services of the top political advertising agencies to create slick spots.

Jay, however, had been wrong about the mood of the people. He'd thought that enough of them had felt hopeless and disenchanted to insure his election. Instead, he found that his views were far too liberal for the exceptionally conservative district. The voters liked the cautious way Dodge had been representing them in the House.

In fact, Dodge had done little in his first term that was likely to offend anyone. He had spent his time studying the internal politics on Capitol Hill until he knew exactly how to get things done. He had learned to play the games necessary to assure passage of pet legislation, but he had never compromised his integrity on the issues, at least as far as Stacy had been able to discover.

Goodness knows, she had tried to find some flaw in his record that she could exploit in Jay's favor. Stacy searched hard for signs of a shady deal, kickbacks, or special favors, but there had been none. He had voted his conscience every time, even when it had gone against his party and the Washington power brokers, who could have helped him achieve a national reputation.

Reluctantly, Stacy had found herself admiring the man, despite the clash of their political views. He seemed real in a world she had rapidly discovered was filled with artificiality. More important, he actually seemed to care about the people in his district, even those with whom he couldn't possibly have much in common. His stands on economic issues had been devastating to the poor, but she had come to realize that he honestly felt they represented the only route toward any sort of long-term solution to the country's problems.

Ironically, the more convinced she became of Dodge's honesty, the more she questioned her faith in Jay. Even though she shared his more liberal point-of-view on most issues, she realized that his convictions were superficial, capable of being swayed by the merest shift in public opinion. Maybe some of what she was feeling now about this assignment was guilt, a feeling that she had betrayed her own conscience by sticking with a candidate in whom she no longer believed.

By the time she reached her high-rise apartment complex across the Potomac River in Arlington, she was beginning to look forward to doing the documentary. She still had her qualms about the conflict of interest inherent in her being given the assignment in the first place, but there was a challenge that a good reporter couldn't resist. It would be fascinating to put Dodge, with all of his intriguing contradictions, under a microscope and dissect him for the public.

Upstairs, she opened the sliding door to her tiny balcony to let in the spring breeze. The apartment was only partially furnished. She'd picked out a sofa and matching chair in dark brown and a huge, glass-topped coffee table, but that was it so far for the living room. The television was sitting on top of several boxes she had yet to unpack. Stacy sighed at the thought of all she had left to do to make the place seem like home. Yet she couldn't tackle it tonight. Dodge was too much on her mind.

Kicking off her shoes, she padded across the plush beige carpet to the bedroom and changed into the old jeans and T-shirt. Then she went straight to her files. Fortunately, she had kept most of her campaign material, when she'd moved back from California.

There might be something among the clippings, position papers and flyers to give her a focus for the documentary. It couldn't be simply a profile of Dodge. No one cared about a second-term Congressman in this town, unless there was something unique to be said about him. The show would need a strong point-of-view, an important issue to make it work. The angle was here somewhere, she hoped, as she sorted through the papers. It had to be.

But, despite hours of reading, she couldn't find it. Tired and dispirited by her lack of success, Stacy picked up a campaign picture of Dodge and studied it, as though in search of clues to reveal his personality. It was a casual picture, unlike most she had seen. His white shirt was mussed and open at the throat, his tie loose. His brown hair was cropped short with just enough curl to hint that it would be unruly at any other length. He looked tan, healthy, and disturbingly virile.

The brown eyes that stared back at her from the picture looked serious, but had the slightest suggestion of a question in them. It was as though he had been contemplating a great puzzle, but had not found the answer, when the photographer had clicked the shutter. There was also something else in those eyes, something that warmed her in an irrational way that scared her.

For the first time, she realized that the danger in this assignment might not have anything to do with her previous ties to J.J. Lawrence. She had an instinctive, sensual reaction to Wayne Dodge that she'd never fully acknowledged before. It was an unsettling twist to an already complicated situation.

Two

The next two weeks were among the most frustrating Stacy had ever spent as a reporter. Every day she had tried to arrange an interview with Wayne Dodge and each time she had gotten the runaround from either his secretary or his administrative assistant.

"Congressman Dodge is in a meeting and cannot be disturbed," the secretary had intoned mechanically on several occasions.

"I don't want to speak to him now," Stacy had insisted. "I just want to schedule an appointment."

"Then you'll have to speak with his assistant, John Temple."

"Fine. Is Mr. Temple there?"

"No. I'm sorry. He's with the Congressman and can't be disturbed."

It seemed to be a vicious circle with no end in sight. Finally, after one entirely wasted week, she had reached John Temple.

"I'm terribly sorry, Miss Allen, but the Congressman will be tied up for at least a week. He is drafting an important piece of legislation and there are hearings to attend. I'm sure you understand," he had said smoothly.

"No, I don't understand at all," Stacy had snapped, her patience worn thin by the constant excuses. "I would probably have less trouble getting in touch with the President. Is Congressman Dodge busier than he is?"

John Temple was irritatingly calm throughout her tirade. "Please, don't get upset. I'm sure we'll be able to arrange something for you in the near future. Why don't you call back in a week or so?"

"I trust your boss is more responsive to his constituents than he is to the media or he'll have a very short career in Washington, Mr. Temple. I warn you that I will do this documentary with or without your assistance. If you wish to have the Congressman appear aloof, unattainable and secretive, that's up to you. Personally, I doubt it'll do much for his image."

With that she had slammed down the phone, knowing that her threat bore little substance and that it had probably only further antagonized John Temple.

For several days she was absorbed with this preliminary background work. It was a little like gathering the pieces of a puzzle. As soon as she had them all, she would be able to put together a picture of the whole man. Until she could see Dodge, she would have to interview those who knew him.

She sought out other members of the California delegation, many of whom had clashed with him over legislation affecting the state. She spoke to high-ranking Republicans who shared his party politics and his views, and to liberal Democrats who found him to be a tough, but fair-minded opponent.

She was unable to learn much about his private life. She went to the posh section of Georgetown, where ivy trailed over his brick townhouse, and met his neighbors. They described him as a pleasant, quiet man, who seldom socialized. There wasn't a hint that he was taking any advantage of being an available man in a town that put a premium on eligible bachelors.

The pieces of the puzzle were beginning to fit, but the picture that was emerging had more shadows and gray areas in it than distinctive images in black-and-white. Only Wayne Dodge himself could bring the proper lighting to the picture. She had to find a way to see him. Judging from the attitude of his staff, his office door was likely to remain closed to her indefinitely. A confrontation in the hallway of the House would accomplish nothing.

She was contemplating this dilemma after work one night, when Paul Robbins, another of the station's reporters, joined her in the bar of a restaurant down the block from the station.

"Is this a private gloom or can anyone join in?" he asked.

Stacy looked up with a welcoming smile. "Frankly, I'm glad of the company. Have a seat and I'll try to cheer up for you."

"That's not necessary on my account. I can probably match your mood. It's been a lousy day."

Stacy studied his face for a moment and realized he wasn't joking. Paul Robbins was a 35-year-old medical reporter with whom she'd been out a couple of times on casual dates. There were no real sparks between them and they both knew it.

There was real concern in her voice now, as she asked, "What happened today? Rough story?"

Paul was silent for several minutes, his head buried in his hands. When he looked up at last, his expression was solemn and shaken.

"The worst. A little girl, the cutest thing you ever saw had a kidney transplant a few weeks ago. Looked as though she would make out just fine. She'd been in the hospital for months waiting for the donor. Her mother told authorities she couldn't cope with the bills or the care, so she walked right out of the kid's life."

"That's awful," Stacy said softly.

"Yeah. Well, I can't blame the mother too much. She had five other kids, little income, no husband. It was an impossible situation for her. Anyway, that's when I got to know Becky. I did a story about her, about how much trouble officials were having finding a foster home for her. Finally, they found a family and Becky went home. She was the happiest kid you ever saw." His voice trailed off.

"What happened?"

"They're not sure. Probably a rejection. Whatever it is, she's back in the hospital. I just came from seeing her. She looks so pitiful lying there in that great big bed. She's trying so hard to be brave. It tears me up. She's so little and so alone."

Stacy's voice was choked with emotion, as she took his hand and whispered, "Paul, I'm so sorry. Maybe she'll pull through again. She did before."

"Maybe," Paul said doubtfully. "But where will she go this time? Her family doesn't want her. She's right back where she started."

"It'll work out. She's got you on her side, doesn't she?"

"Thanks," he said, squeezing her hand. "I'm not sure that's enough."

He was silent for a minute, then said, "I don't know how these doctors do it, handling stuff like this. It wipes me out."

"Maybe they don't handle it as well as you think they do. They may have outlets you know nothing about. They may go home and punch holes in a wall or slam a racketball around, until it's all out of their system. They're no stronger than you are, Paul. They've just found a way to cope."

"Maybe I should change jobs, become a consumer reporter," Paul suggested with a hint of a smile. "Maybe I wouldn't feel so much compassion for a guy who's trying to bilk the average housewife out of her savings."

"Probably not, but you'd hate it, though," Stacy said with certainty.

"I guess I would," he admitted ruefully. "Now, then, what about you? What was that gloomy look I saw on your face all about?"

"Nothing terribly important, really. Just a reluctant subject."

Quickly she outlined her assignment and her difficulty in getting to Wayne Dodge.

"I was just debating what my next step should be, when you came along."

"Your solution's a lot easier than you think."

"Okay, expert. What should I do?"

"Why not walk into the dining room, sit down at his table and ask him for an interview," he suggested casually, laughing at her incredulous expression.

"He's here?"

"Yep. Walked in with a gorgeous lady about fifteen minutes ago. I'm surprised you didn't notice. I thought he was the sort of man that made you women go all weak."

"I haven't gone all weak over a man, since Warren Beatty kissed my cheek at a fundraising party in California."

"Warren Beatty, huh? No wonder I didn't have a chance."

"Seriously, Paul, do you really think I should go in there and butt in on Wayne Dodge's date?"

"Public figures don't have much claim to privacy in the middle of a restaurant. Seems to me you'll never have a better chance of getting him to agree to an interview."

"Okay," she said, getting to her feet and moving reluctantly toward the dining room. As she entered, she took one last look back at Paul for reassurance. Then she scanned the dimly-lit room in search of Dodge and his companion. At last she spotted them in a corner booth, deep in animated conversation. Bracing herself, she approached the table.

"Excuse me, Congressman."

Startled, he looked up at her, his eyes traveling from her cap of curls down to the violet eyes fringed with thick lashes, then to the full, pink lips, the trim figure in the gray suit. His brazen survey heightened the color in her cheeks.

"Yes," he said with polite curiosity, a slight smile tugging at the corners of his mouth. "Surely you're not our waitress?"

"Hardly," she said tersely, her nervousness increased by the intensity of his gaze. She had been unprepared for the sheer magnetism of the man, for the sudden knotting of her stomach muscles as her eyes met his.

"I . . . I'm Stacy Allen," she managed at last, furious that he seemed to leave her tongue-tied and ill at ease.

"Well, Stacy Allen, what can I do for you?"

"I would like to make an appointment to see you, Congressman."

"Oh? I should think that would be easy enough to arrange. You're a very attractive young lady."

Stacy was infuriated by the amusement in his voice, but she was determined to keep a tight rein on her temper.

"This isn't personal, Mr. Dodge," she said stiffly, deliberately dropping the respectful title of Congressman.

"That's too bad," he said with feigned sorrow, ignoring his date's growing irritation and Stacy's anger. "I was rather hoping it was."

"Sorry to disappoint you, but it's strictly professional."

"Just what profession are you in, Miss Allen?" he asked, his mocking tone suggesting he doubted it could be anything terribly important.

"I'm a reporter."

"Well, Stacy Allen, reporter, why don't you sit down for a minute and tell me what you need?"

Stacy sensed that he was still making fun of her, but she forced herself to ignore his attitude. What did it matter as long as he agreed to the interview?

"I really am sorry to intrude," she apologized. "I've been trying to reach you for several weeks now. Your associates are very protective."

She was unable to keep the resentment from her voice and Wayne Dodge picked up on it immediately. His manner was serious when he told her, "Apparently, I owe you an apology then, Miss Allen. Sometimes my staff guards me a little too well. If I agreed to see everyone who'd like a minute or two of my time, I'd be totally ineffective in Congress. But they're supposed to use better judgment. I always agree to see members of the media."

"I'm glad to hear that, because I need to arrange for some time with you. I've been assigned to do a documentary about you for my station, an in-depth profile about who you are, some of your stands, your political future, that sort of thing. I've done most of the background work, but now I need your cooperation."

"So," he said slowly, nodding as if in sudden understanding. "You're the one." Gone in an instant was the friendly, bantering tone, the charming look. It had been replaced by a dawning of icy disdain.

"The one what?" Stacy asked, puzzled by the sudden change.

"The woman who has been asking all the questions," he said, biting off each word. "Several people have mentioned you. You're apparently quite thorough."

From the look on his face, Stacy could see that he didn't mean it as a compliment.

"Unfortunately," he continued, "none of them recognized you as a local reporter, so a few of them assumed you were either a phony or perhaps an FBI investigator."

"You're kidding?" Stacy said in amazement. "But I identified myself."

"Perhaps you did, Miss Allen, but the paranoia in this community runs deep. Surely you understand that. Everyone is sure they're under surveillance of one sort or another or that their neighbors are. I can tell you that I've spent a couple of damned uncomfortable weeks, thanks to your snooping."

Drawing herself up indignantly, Stacy said, "I was not snooping, as you put it."

"What would you call it?"

"I was doing my job. I'm a reporter, Congressman."

"Reporters snoop, Miss Allen. It's the nature of the business. I'm not naive. As a Congressman, I know that my public life will be subjected to every sort of scrutiny, but I'll be damned if I'll allow you or anyone else to invade my private life."

"It's all part of the same man. It takes both sides together to present a picture of the whole Wayne Dodge. You must understand that?"

"You're the one who needs to understand something, Miss Allen. You will have to make do with half of Wayne Dodge, because my Congressional record and performance is all you'll investigate with any cooperation from me or anyone in my office. If you can be satisfied with that, call my assistant for an appointment. I'll see to it that he arranges one for you. However," he added, his voice taking on a warning edge, "if you speak to a single one of my neighbors or friends again, I'll see to it that you not only lose your story, but your job as well. Do I make myself clear?"

"Perfectly," Stacy said coldly, knowing she could only comply with his wishes at this point. "I will speak to your assistant tomorrow."

Although she was shaking with anger, she held her shoulders back and her head high, as she walked away from the table. She had gone only a few feet, when Wayne Dodge's voice called out to her in a tone that commanded she turn around. Reluctantly, she faced him.

"I'll be looking forward to our next meeting," he said softly, his expression amused as he saw her clench her hands at her sides.

Seething with unexpressed anger, she joined Paul.

"How did it go?" he asked. "Not too well, judging from the look on your face. Wouldn't he agree to see you?"

"Oh, he agreed to see me. But he is the most impossible, arrogant, demanding man I have ever met. He insists that the only way I will get any help from him or his staff is if I stay entirely away from his personal life."

"What do you suppose he's hiding?" Paul asked, instantly curious.

Stacy stared at him, reluctant to admit that she'd wondered the same thing. "Why do you assume that he has to be hiding something?"

"Isn't that what you think?"

"I don't know what to think. Maybe he's just being

difficult, because the people I've already interviewed have been giving him a rough time about it."

"Maybe," Paul agreed. "But at least you've got your interview. Why don't we celebrate? Stay and have dinner with me."

Relieved that she wouldn't have to spend the evening alone with her uncomfortable doubts about Wayne Dodge, she agreed readily. "I'd love to."

Paul settled their bar bill and they moved into the dining room, where, unfortunately, the only available table was just a few yards from the one where Dodge and his date were enjoying their dinner. Stacy balked at being in close proximity to him so soon after their confrontation.

"Paul, why don't we go somewhere else?"

"Why?" he asked. Then he followed her gaze. "You mean because of Dodge? Don't be crazy, Stacy. He's not paying the least bit of attention to you. With that blonde beside him, you're the last thing on his mind."

Stacy wasn't sure which bothered her more, the accuracy of Paul's assessment of the situation or her own jealous reaction to the way in which Wayne Dodge and his companion were staring at each other.

"Okay," she agreed. "We'll stay."

But despite her decision to remain and make the best of an awkward situation, she was unable to keep her mind on her own date, the juicy rare steaks he had insisted on ordering, or the fine, dry red wine.

Instead, she seemed to be conscious only of those inquisitive brown eyes across the room, as they repeatedly strayed from the lovely companion at his side to seek out Stacy. Once, when he caught her returning his gaze, the corners of his mouth had lifted in the slightest flicker of a smile.

"Damn him," she swore softly, furious that he

seemed to be able to read her mind and that he found it amusing.

Puzzled by her exclamation, Paul asked, "Stacy, what is it now?"

"Paul, I'm sorry. I know I'm not being very good company. I can't seem to keep my mind on anything tonight. Maybe I should just go on home."

As she said that, a shadow loomed over the table and she looked up to find Wayne Dodge towering over her. His lithe six-foot one-inch frame was muscled and fit under his well-tailored suit. That fluttering in the pit of her stomach began again.

"I just wanted to stop and say good night, Miss Allen. Enjoy the rest of your dinner."

His smooth politeness was as infuriating as the amusement Stacy could read beneath the surface of his remarks. Before she could reply, he had gone, leaving her trembling.

Paul took her hand and held it tightly as he said, "I know you didn't ask for my advice, babe, but I'm going to offer some anyway. Watch your step with the Congressman."

"What do you mean?" Stacy asked defensively.

"You know exactly what I mean. You're getting in way over your head. It's obvious from the way you look at the man."

Stacy sighed. "You're right, Paul. I'll be careful. I know the rules of this business."

Three

Stacy sat on the Victorian sofa, with its richly-textured brocade upholstery, and studied her surroundings. One wall was filled with books from floor to ceiling. A modern painting, in soft, pastel tones that hinted of the sea, hung over the fireplace. As lovely as it was, it seemed incongruous among all the antiques in the room.

A pile of reading material was stacked haphazardly on the table to her left, including everything from issues of the *Congressional Record* and a collection of political essays to a rare first edition of *Alice in Wonderland*.

Intrigued by the inclusion of the latter, she picked the book up and thumbed through it, delighting in the colorful illustrations. On the flyleaf, in a bold handwriting, someone named Jennifer had scrawled, "In anticipation of our next tea party." A twinge of jealousy over the inscription's suggested intimacy made Stacy slam the book shut.

She was still holding the book, when she heard Wayne Dodge's deep-throated chuckle behind her.

With the stinging accusation that she was "nothing more than a snoop" still ringing in her mind from their last encounter, she blushed at being caught with the book in her hand. She returned it to the stack on the table with shaking hands, knocking off several other books and papers in the process. Dodge seemed to find this even more amusing.

"Sorry," she mumbled, getting down on the floor to retrieve the scattered items.

"Don't worry about it," a husky voice said close to her ear, as a hand reached out to stay hers. "It might as well stay down here. That's where it was before you arrived. The maid gathered it up, thinking it would make a better impression. She's still intimidated by the media."

He sounded as though the thought of such intimidation struck him as absurd.

"And you're not intimidated?" Stacy inquired in a sweetly sarcastic voice. "That's certainly not the impression you gave the other night."

"Intimidated? Never," he said firmly. "I merely resent reporters prying into areas that are none of their concern. Besides," he added, his gaze roving lazily over her body, "I could never be intimidated by someone as lovely as you."

"Perhaps you should be. I'm tougher than I look."

"I don't doubt it, Miss Allen. Your persistence has already proved that. I promise to take you seriously."

Stacy searched his face for a mocking expression, but found none. "Then, will you answer a question for me?"

"I thought that was what this interview was all about," he retorted grinning. "You ask the questions. I give the answers. Isn't that how it works?"

"This one has nothing to do with the documentary. At least not directly."

"Oh?" he asked suspiciously. "Well, try me anyway. If I don't like it, I can always refuse to comment."

"It's nothing that controversial," she assured him. "I just wondered why you agreed to see me at your home after everything you said the other night about privacy."

He gave her a considering look, before responding slowly, "I suppose it was to prove to you that I have nothing to hide. That is what you were thinking, isn't it?"

Although she said nothing, Stacy knew her momentary hesitation had given her away.

"I thought so," he said, acknowledging that her actions had confirmed his fears. "I knew my defensiveness had given you the wrong impression. Besides," he added with a shrug, "we won't be interrupted here. We'd never get anything accomplished at my office."

Stacy nodded. "Fair enough. Could I ask one personal question, though, before we get started?"

"Ask."

"Tell me about the book."

"What book?"

"*Alice in Wonderland.* It seems an odd choice for you."

He laughed then, a booming, joyous sound that took Stacy by surprise. She had seen evidence that he found a certain cynical amusement in life, but this was the first proof she'd had that he had a sense of humor that wasn't at someone else's expense.

"It's not as odd as you think. Did you read the inscription?"

"That's what made me curious," she admitted.

"The young lady who gave me the book . . ."

"Jennifer."

"Yes. Jennifer was referring to a party we'd been

to at the home of a very influential lobbyist. She said it reminded her of the Mad Hatter's tea party."

Stacy joined in his laughter. "That's typical of a lot of Washington functions, isn't it? I don't suppose you'd want to reveal which lobbyist it was?"

"Not on your life. Gossip like that can only come back to haunt you in this town."

For several seconds there was silence, as Stacy tried to find the right question to launch the interview.

Maddeningly, Dodge seemed to find a certain enjoyment in watching her flounder. He had settled in a chair across from her, his long legs stretched out in front of him, a glint of amusement in his brown eyes. Stacy couldn't decide whether she wanted to slap that look from his face or feel those hard, muscular arms around her. Flustered by the warmth that seemed to radiate through her body at the thought of being in his arms, she groped frantically for the first question that came to mind.

"You have a lovely home here. Did you use a decorator?" Inwardly she winced at the innocuous beginning, but Dodge seemed to take the remark at face value.

"Thanks. I feel more at home here now than I do at my place in California. I've spent most of the last two years tracking down the right antiques. Most of the rooms are just about finished."

"You did this yourself?" Stacy said, unable to keep the astonishment from her voice. The thought of Wayne Dodge haunting antique shops and auctions seemed almost as incongruous as if he'd told her he'd spent a year hunting wild game in Africa. It didn't fit with his three-piece-suit image.

She looked around with new interest, appreciating more than ever the warm blending of colors and the gleaming wood. The wide planked floors were bare except for a few scattered Oriental carpets in tones muted by years of wear. Although the fireplace wasn't in use on this warm spring evening, she could imagine what a cozy room it would be on a cold winter night. Tonight, however, the French doors that led to a small brick patio were open and the scent of lilacs drifted in.

"Would you like to see the rest?" Dodge invited eagerly. "I have some terrific pieces upstairs."

"Are you sure you trust me enough to show me through your home?" Stacy asked, feeling suddenly lighthearted about his willingness to show her around.

But her reference to his concern with privacy immediately altered the friendly atmosphere that had been growing between them. His voice stiffened with politeness as he said, "As I told you, Miss Allen, I have nothing to hide. If you're really interested, I'd be delighted to show you the house. If you'd rather not spend the time doing so, we can get on with your questions."

Quickly trying to salvage the mood, Stacy said, "No, please, I'd love to look around."

As they wandered from room to room, Dodge's excitement was contagious and Stacy found herself asking about each table and cabinet just to hear him talk about where he'd found it and what he'd learned of its history.

"You really enjoy the hunting as much as the possessing, don't you?"

"Absolutely. There's no better way to spend a weekend than driving through the country, finding out-of-the-way shops to dig around in, having a cup of coffee with the dealers. People who sell antiques love to talk. They're the ones who tell me what the folks outside of Washington really think about things. They reflect the mood of the people more accurately than any poll I've ever seen."

"Sounds like fun," Stacy said sincerely.

Wayne paused and looked deeply into her eyes, as though to confirm something he'd sensed in her voice. Although his gaze was filled with meaning, his tone was casual as he suggested, "Why don't you come with me sometime? There's a farm sale in Maryland next weekend. How about it?"

Stacy hesitated as the memory of Paul's warning about involvement echoed in her mind. Finally she managed to convince herself that this would be an extraordinary opportunity to glimpse another side of Wayne Dodge. "Sounds great," she agreed at last.

Back downstairs, they found that the maid had left them a pot of coffee and a tray of sandwiches. For the next three hours, Stacy worked her way through the complex maze of Wayne Dodge's mind. She was surprised to find that he was open and straightforward, no matter how deeply she probed. He talked about his days at boarding school when he'd felt lonely and isolated from his family, his uneasy relationship with his parents, and his undergraduate and law school days at Harvard.

The stories were told in a flat, even voice, devoid of anger. But Stacy sensed there were certain emotions just beneath the surface, scars that needed protection because they had not yet fully healed.

As though afraid he might be revealing too much, he changed the subject, moving on to his career with a prestigious Los Angeles law firm. He'd joined the firm right after his graduation from Harvard, but it hadn't taken him long to realize that he'd made a mistake. Conflicts had arisen immediately.

"What sort of conflicts?" Stacy asked.

"Pounced right on that, didn't you? There may be a bit of the scandalmonger in you after all, Stacy Allen," he teased.

"You brought it up," she said defensively.

"So I did," he agreed with a grin that made her heart flop over. "Okay, then. My partners, Gerald Williams and Allan Michaelson, are fine lawyers. They built that firm up from a two-man office into a legal octopus with tentacles reaching into every kind of law . . . corporate, taxes, divorce. You name it and someone there specialized in it. I was very fortunate to be accepted into the fold right out of college. Other lawyers with far more experience would have killed for the opportunity I was given."

"But you didn't want it," Stacy guessed.

Dodge nodded. "I hated it. The cases were all too clean and tidy. They handled only the wealthiest clients, the men and women who could afford the best, people like my parents.

"They didn't want to dirty their reputation by taking on some poor, unemployed man whose landlord had just evicted him from a one-room apartment without heat or electricity. Or the migrant laborer, who hadn't been paid a dime for three months of work, because his employer claimed there was nothing left after he'd deducted the rent for the shack he'd been allowed to live in and for his bill at the company store.

"If you ask me, these are the people who need help the most, but the only place they ever get it is from some legal aid attorney, who is usually young, inexperienced and overworked. He doesn't have a prayer against the system. Send in a high-powered lawyer from a firm like ours and at least there's a chance some sort of justice will be done."

Dodge spoke with a passionate conviction that demonstrated why he'd been regarded as an eloquent speaker on the campaign circuit. As Stacy studied the look of intensity and compassion on his face, she realized what a truly remarkable man he was. These traits made him a powerful adversary, as well as a potently attractive man.

"What did you do about the way you felt?"

He grinned. "I took the cases anyway. Oh, just a couple. Not enough to jeopardize the firm's reputation, but at least it was a start. When it finally began to rankle too much, they suggested I take a leave of absence and go into politics. I agreed. I thought maybe I could do more good that way."

His mouth curved in an ironic twist. "Isn't idealism wonderful? I'm in my second term now and I don't think I've accomplished a damn thing."

"Of course you have," Stacy contradicted him indignantly. "What about the legislation protecting migrant labor from exploitation and the law to close down the smuggling of illegal aliens from Mexico by those sweat shop owners?"

"I see you've done your homework," he said approvingly. "But there's a great distance between proposing a piece of legislation and actually getting it approved and then enforced."

"You'll manage it," she said with certainty. "I've seen how well you've gotten to know the political system on the Hill. It's something some newcomers never learn. But you have and you'll find the support you need."

"Thanks for the vote of confidence," he said, his voice suddenly husky as he allowed his gaze to roam over her body. A tension, born of sudden sexual awareness, filled the room. "You are a most unusual woman, Stacy Allen," he said quietly.

"And you are . . ." she began, her voice trailing off, as she forced herself not to complete the thought.

"I am what?" he persisted.

"Nothing," she said abruptly, trying to end the discussion. "I shouldn't have said anything."

Gathering up her notebook, pen, and other papers,

she stuffed them hurriedly into her briefcase. "It's late. I really must be going."

Moving toward the door, she told him, "I really do appreciate all the time you've spent with me."

Hands stuffed in his pockets, he followed her at a leisurely pace that seemed to mock her sudden rush.

"It's been a surprising pleasure," he conceded. "You're easy to talk to. That's probably why you're a good journalist. People find themselves opening up to you without even realizing it and pretty soon they're revealing all their deep, dark secrets."

"You haven't revealed any so far."

"Disappointed?" he asked in a teasing tone. "Maybe that'll keep you coming back for more."

"Oh, I'll be back," she agreed. "You don't think I'm through with you yet, do you?"

"I hope not," he said, his gaze revealing a new intensity. In one long stride he was beside her, a hand reaching out to gently trace the fullness of her lips. Stacy's body shivered at his touch.

Then a powerful arm had encircled her waist, pulling her against the full length of him. His lips, descending slowly to meet hers, had barely made contact before she was pulling away. Breathless, she was fighting to maintain her composure, unwilling to let him see how shaken she was by the fleeting contact.

Trying to inject a note of professional dignity into her voice, she said shakily, "Thank . . . Thank you again for your time, Congressman."

Ignoring her retreat behind a facade of politeness, he insisted, "Wayne, please."

Drawing her back into his embrace, he continued, "Come on. Say it, Stacy Allen. Wayne. I want to hear you say it."

"Wayne," she whispered at last, abandoning any

pretense of uninvolvement. A tiny gasp escaped as his lips touched the sensitive skin of her neck.

"Congressman, please," she said urgently. "This is crazy."

"Isn't it?" he agreed with impossible calmness. "I can't recall feeling quite this way in a very long time."

His hands were moving slowly, sensuously over her body as he spoke. It was a hypnotic combination and Stacy had no power or will to resist.

"You are an incredibly beautiful woman," he said huskily. "You're bright, sensitive, funny."

Each compliment was punctuated by a kiss, gentle, undemanding assaults that left Stacy's knees weak. Had he not been holding her so tightly, she wasn't sure she could have continued to stand.

"I think I may be falling in love with you, Stacy Allen," he said and his voice held a note of surprise and awe.

But Stacy was unaware of the tone. She heard only his words. It was absurd, she thought. What on earth was he trying to prove with such a ridiculous declaration? Every protective instinct in her rallied to create an almost irrational anger. No one fell in love at first sight except in novels! She jerked herself from his arms, shaking with rage.

"How dare you?" she shouted in unrestrained fury, as Wayne stared at her as though she had suddenly gone mad.

"What on earth is wrong?" he asked, genuinely puzzled by her anger.

"You know very well what's wrong," she replied icily. "How dare you try to seduce me?"

Wayne's face became cold and expressionless. "Do you find that thought so distasteful?" he asked in a voice thick with sarcasm. "I'm afraid your body betrayed you, my dear. You want me as much as I want you."

"No," Stacy insisted, though the memory of how his touch had stirred her made her shiver involuntarily.

"Yes," he said softly, taking a step toward her.

Stacy backed out of his reach. "No, damn it. You're only trying to seduce me so I'll drop the story. You know I'd have to drop it, if I slept with you."

"Good God, where did you come up with that idea?" he asked in amazement. "The thought never crossed my mind. You are being utterly absurd, Stacy."

"Am I really? Or are you trying to make sure that whatever it is you have to hide remains hidden?"

"So, we're back to that," he said resignedly. "All right, you believe what you like, Miss Allen, but I see no point in continuing this discussion. Why don't you leave before we both say some more things we don't mean?"

Stacy stared at him miserably, becoming even more ashamed of her behavior at the look of derision she saw on his face. She knew she had overreacted, but she couldn't admit it. She just couldn't. She wheeled and headed for her car. As she neared it, he called out to her.

"The farm sale is at noon on Sunday. I'll pick you up at ten o'clock."

Astonished that he still intended for them to go out, she turned back to refuse. But he had gone inside and closed the door.

Four

When the doorbell rang promptly at ten A.M. Sunday, Stacy still had not resolved her conflicting emotions about Wayne. The memory of his declaration of love taunted her. What if he had been telling the truth? It could only lead to disaster, professional and, just as likely, personal. Besides, it couldn't be true. He barely knew her.

Oh, he wanted her all right. There was no doubt about that. But that was something else entirely. Chemistry. Lust. Whatever you wanted to call it, it had nothing to do with love.

The doorbell rang again, but she couldn't bring herself to answer. It was her pride, as much as anything, that kept her huddled in a corner of the sofa. She was still furious that he had arrogantly assumed she would go meekly along with him today, despite their argument. Stubbornly, she sat there, listening to the insistent buzzing. Finally she heard Wayne's footsteps quietly retreating down the hallway.

"That takes care of that," she thought, but there was little satisfaction in knowing that she'd gotten even with him. Deep down she realized she was behaving like a spoiled child or, more damning still, like a foolish woman who might be falling in love.

With the mournful melodies of a jazz album to set the mood, she stayed curled up on the sofa and thought once more about trying to get Pete to put someone else on the story. But, she rationalized, she had already tried that once and Pete had refused to listen to any of her pleas. He was unlikely to be any more receptive to her arguments now, unless she admitted that she was falling in love with Wayne. That might shake him enough to change his mind, but the admission would cost her more than she was willing to pay.

So, she was stuck. She would have to do the best she could to get her emotions under control. If she completed the documentary as rapidly as possible, that would be the end of it. No more conflict of interest and no more Wayne Dodge to torment her. After refusing to answer the door this morning, he'd probably never even speak to her again, though.

"Damn," she muttered aloud. "Why did I behave so stupidly? He'll probably be furious and then where will I be with the story?"

Deciding that a walk on the mild spring morning might clear her head, she grabbed a jacket and her purse and left the apartment. As she turned the corner toward the elevator, a tall shadow darkened the wall in front of her. Startled, she let out a muffled yelp and sped back toward her apartment. But before she could run more than a few yards, a hand clenched her arm in a tight, unrelenting grip.

"Not so quickly, young lady," the familiar, deep voice said sternly.

She spun around straight into the arms of Wayne Dodge.

"You!" she gasped, her eyes widening. "But . . . I thought . . ."

"You thought I'd crept away with my tail tucked between my legs, like some puppy you'd chastised. You should know me better than that."

"Yes," she agreed, her eyes downcast. Then curiosity got the better of her. "Why didn't you leave?"

"Because we had a date and I couldn't believe that you would actually stand me up."

"That's rather an arrogant assumption, don't you think?"

"Actually, it has less to do with my faith in my fatal charm than my belief in you."

"In me?"

"Yes. I was sure you wouldn't be that childish. Perhaps I was wrong, after all." There was a questioning look in his eyes, as he studied her. She was unable to meet that gaze.

At last she said quietly, "I'm sorry. I really am. It was a ridiculous thing to do."

"Does that mean you're ready to come along with me now?"

Stacy hesitated only an instant, then nodded.

"Then let's get going before we miss all the good stuff," he said, his mood instantly shifting now that she had apologized and agreed to come along.

Somehow she found his ability to change emotional gears irritating. He seemed to take a smug satisfaction in getting his own way, too.

"Let it go," she warned herself, keeping her mouth shut as she followed him to the elevator.

In the parking lot she was surprised to find him approaching a beat-up station wagon, several years old and badly in need of waxing. Noticing her incredulous look, he laughed.

"Not what you expected the wealthy, bachelor Congressman to be driving, is it?"

"Not exactly," Stacy conceded.

"Never fear. I have the requisite sports car, though I'm sorry to tell you it isn't a flashy red. It's also not nearly large enough to haul around antique chests and brass beds. This one is more practical for these hunting expeditions."

She realized she was discovering a totally unexpected side to Wayne. His clothes, for instance. He was dressed today in a manner she would have once thought to be totally out of character. His jeans were so worn in spots they were practically threadbare and they were the basic, durable jeans of a rancher, rather than the fancy designer variety. His plaid shirt could have come from a catalog. Only his boots had the expensive sheen of good leather and fancy Texas styling. Oddly enough, he looked perfectly natural, as though he'd have been as comfortable cleaning out a horse stall, as he was at those $100-a-plate formal dinners.

He also looked disturbingly masculine. Somehow his shoulders seemed broader, more muscular in the soft, blue plaid material of his shirt. The open collar revealed a mat of crisp, dark hairs on his chest. Stacy had an almost irresistible urge to reach out and touch their roughness, to feel the warm skin beneath. As though afraid she might yield to the urge, she slid slightly closer to her door.

For nearly half an hour they rode in silence, as Wayne guided the car through the Sunday traffic onto the beltway that would take them around Washington and into Maryland. Once they'd passed through the worst of the traffic, he reached over to the glove compartment in front of her to rummage through some tapes. When he'd selected one and inserted it into the car stereo, Stacy realized he'd chosen the same haunting Stanley Turrentine album she'd been playing earlier at home.

"Why, that's . . ." Suddenly, she looked closely at him and realized he was chuckling softly. "You heard it, didn't you? You knew all along that I was at home," she accused indignantly.

He nodded, keeping his eyes straight ahead, as though afraid to look at her. "You must have been lousy at hide and seek, when you were a kid," he observed wryly.

"As a matter of fact, I was," she admitted, laughing with him. "How long were you planning to sit out in the hall?"

"As long as it took to get you to come out. I'd have been back to ring the bell again in another few minutes."

"You're a very patient man."

He gave her a quick look. "Very," he drawled. "Especially when the stakes are high."

When Stacy didn't respond, he asked lightly, "Want to tell me why you didn't answer the first time? You weren't still angry about the other day, were you?"

"That was part of it," she conceded.

"And the rest?"

"It's . . . it's nothing I can talk about."

"Why on earth not?" he asked impatiently, then promptly tempered his tone. "If it has to do with me, don't you think I have a right to know?"

"Probably. But I can't talk about it. Please. Maybe someday, but not now."

He shook his head. "Stacy, we can't solve problems, if we don't talk about them."

"I know," she murmured so softly, he thought for a moment she hadn't responded at all. Stealing a glance at her, he saw the mixture of pain and confusion on her face.

"Okay," he said, reaching over to pat her hand. "I won't ask again. When you're ready, you tell me. Deal?"

"Deal," she agreed gratefully. Perhaps someday she would be able to explain to him this sense she had of being on an emotional Ferris wheel ride, one minute swinging wildly, ecstatically at the top, and the next minute sinking to the bottom, desperate to get off.

Outside the car, which Wayne drove with confident ease, the crowded cityscape was giving way to rolling fields. When they left the highway and began winding along a narrow, country road, Stacy felt as though she were back home in Ohio.

"This is heavenly," she said, breathing deeply to savor the pungent mix of scents. "Sometimes I forget how much I miss it."

"You grew up in the country?"

"Is that so hard to believe?" she asked, smiling at his surprise.

"Yes. You seem so much a part of Washington. You're not at all intimidated by it. I thought surely you had grown up there or, at the very least, some other big city."

"Nope. My town would have fit nicely in one tiny corner of Washington. It was in a fairly rural area about forty miles south of Columbus. When I was a kid it was a really big event to get to go to the city to shop or see a play."

Suddenly overcome by nostalgia, she recalled how many Sundays her family had spent just like this, riding through the countryside.

"I remember a game we used to play, when we'd go for rides like this," Stacy told Wayne. "We'd bet on when the first signs of a season would appear—the first crocuses or new leaves in the spring, the first ripe tomatoes in summer, the gold and red leaves in the fall, the first snow."

"I missed all of that in Southern California. That's probably why I enjoy it so much here. Of course,

California does have a change of seasons, but the signs aren't nearly so attractive. Summer's marked by the heat and the dry Santa Ana winds. Winter has rain and mud slides. The smog's there all the time."

"I remember," Stacy said. "It can be pretty horrible."

"You lived in California?" Wayne said, giving her a puzzled glance. "When?"

Mentally Stacy chided herself for making such a stupid slip. She didn't dare tell him now about working for Jay. He'd never understand why she hadn't told him that. More important, he'd no longer trust her. How could he? Jay had been a tough adversary and she had been Jay's right arm.

She hedged now, telling him only, "I did my graduate work at UCLA, then spent a year or so in Los Angeles after that."

"Did you work for one of the stations?"

"Briefly, as a producer. I wasn't on the air at all."

"Did you like Los Angeles?"

"No. I couldn't wait to come back to the East Coast. My real love is politics and this is the place to be for that. California has its own unique brand of politics, but the decisions that really matter are made in Washington."

Stacy realized that she was practically holding her breath for fear he would pursue the conversation about her stay in California. He seemed intent on exploring every detail. Fortunately, though, at that point they apparently were nearing their destination. Wayne slowed down and studied a newspaper ad listing the address for the farm sale.

"Yep," he said, nodding with satisfaction. "This is it."

He turned the car into a dirt driveway. As they bounced over the rough ground they finally saw a field filled with parked cars. Though there was no sign of the house or the crowd, Stacy could hear the rapid-fire chatter of the auctioneer as he exhorted the bidders to keep the price climbing.

As they walked toward the noise, Wayne took her hand to help her across the rough terrain. It was a casual gesture, but Stacy's heart skipped a beat. Its erratic pace didn't slow to normal again, until he released her hand as they neared the crowd.

They approached a folding card table, which was serving as the registration desk for the sale. Behind it a heavyset man with a ruddy complexion and a broad smile greeted them with enthusiastic familiarity.

"Ah, here you are, Congressman. I just knew we'd be seeing you today. Brought the little woman along this time. How do, ma'am?"

Stacy would have denied the status he'd assumed her to have, but Wayne prevented it by simply changing the subject, asking for a number. As soon as he was assigned a number, they joined the crowd milling around in front of the old, ramshackle farm house. As Stacy looked around, her glance came to rest on a table covered with a checkered cloth and laden with homemade pies and cakes, being sold by the slice. The aroma of fresh coffee from the urns on the table drifted in their direction and she avidly eyed the assortment of baked goods.

Following her gaze, Wayne asked, "Want something to eat?"

"Thanks, yes," she admitted, as her stomach rumbled in agreement.

"Good. Let's grab something and then scout around to see what's for sale."

Moments later, a chunk of tart apple pie in one hand and a paper cup of steaming coffee in the other, Stacy found herself trailing after a man who seemed to have forgotten her existence. He was totally absorbed in examining the rickety furniture scattered over the lawn. Most things seemed in pretty bad shape to her untrained eye. Most were covered with several layers of peeling paint. Wayne seemed to be especially interested in one piece, though. He spent several minutes going over a washstand, now a faded white and apparently several other colors in its past. Its intricate carving was barely discernible through the thick layers of paint.

While Wayne continued to explore, she halted at a table covered with boxes of miscellaneous household items. In one carton there was an old jewelry box with broken hinges and a rip in its fake leather covering. It was jammed with earrings, necklaces, stickpins and broaches. Most were cheap costume jewelry, but there was one delicate broach Stacy fell in love with. Gold filigree surrounded a single tiny diamond. It probably hadn't been expensive, but she could imagine how proud of it the owner must have been. She was holding it in her hand, when Wayne came looking for her.

"I thought I'd lost you," he said, as she replaced the broach in the box.

"I just got sidetracked for a minute."

"Let's go find a place to sit. There are a couple of things I want to bid on."

For the next few hours they sat on hard, metal folding chairs, warmed by the gentle spring sun, as item after item representing a piece of a family's lifetime went up for bids.

Wayne was enjoying every minute of it. He was an experienced bidder and he'd clearly settled on his top price in advance for each item and retreated from the bidding when it was reached. At the end of the afternoon, he'd bought only the washstand.

"Isn't there something you'd like to bid on?" he asked, after the bidding on the washstand ended.

Stacy thought of the delicate broach, but shook her head. "No, nothing."

"Okay. If you're sure, I'll just go pay for the washstand and put it in the car. I'll be back for you in a few minutes."

While he was gone, several boxes from the table were auctioned off, including the jewelry box. Stacy had an urge to bid on it, but decided the emotional appeal of the broach might make her bid far more than it was worth. She watched the bidding proceed with a twinge of envy. Moments after it was over, Wayne returned.

It was nearly dusk by the time they started back. Stacy felt a headache coming on, caused no doubt by the earlier tension and by a lack of food. A piece of pie was hardly filling enough to last for a whole day and she hadn't eaten anything before they'd left in the morning. Absentmindedly she rubbed her aching neck.

Wayne's concern was immediate. "Headache?"

"Just a slight one. It'll go away."

"Tension or hunger?" he persisted.

"A little of both probably."

"Why don't we stop for dinner then? That should take care of half of the problem. Or do you already have plans for this evening?"

"No plans, but wouldn't you rather get home and start working on your latest treasure to see what's underneath all that paint?"

"I already know. It's cherry."

"How can you possibly know that?" Stacy asked in astonishment. "Most of the washstands I've seen are oak."

"Most of them are," he agreed.

"Then why are you so certain this one is cherry?" Wayne looked a bit sheepish before finally admitting, "Because I chipped away some of the paint to look."

"Why you cheat. Here I thought you had some incredible gift of insight that mere amateurs like me couldn't begin to understand."

"I do have a gift," he insisted indignantly.

"Sure!"

"I know enough to look below the surface," he said lightly. There was a sudden warmth in his eyes as he added meaningfully, "That goes for everything . . . including you."

"Oh?"

"Yes," he continued, not taking his eyes from the road. "On the surface, you are cool, professional, very businesslike."

Stacy wasn't sure she liked his analysis, but before she could argue, he went on, "But beneath the surface there's a fire just waiting for someone to ignite it. I want to be the one to do that."

Stacy trembled at the images he had evoked. "I think we'd better talk about something else," she whispered shakily.

"Coward," he responded gently, an unmistakable glint of amusement in his eyes. "What shall we talk about then?"

"How about food?" she suggested meekly. "Where are we going to eat?"

"That's certainly a safe enough topic," he said, grinning broadly at her discomfort. "How's seafood sound?"

"Wonderful."

They drove to a small restaurant along the edge of the Potomac River. Although the atmosphere inside was casual and far from ostentatious, it was a favorite haunt of politicians who were more interested in food than ambiance.

The *maître d'*, recognizing Wayne, took them immediately to a table by the window. It was still fairly early, but already the place was jammed. Their immediate seating drew several angry comments from those who'd been waiting in line. Others only seemed interested in who'd received the preferential treatment. Both reactions made Stacy uncomfortable.

"Shouldn't we have waited our turn?"

Wayne shrugged. "I've been coming here regularly ever since I arrived in Washington. That's the way they treat all their regulars."

To avoid an argument over something that was both ridiculous and out of her control, Stacy studied the menu.

"You want the fancy stuff or are you game for a dozen crabs we can crack ourselves?" Wayne asked after several minutes.

"Let's crack 'em ourselves. I have a feeling that's what relieves most of the tensions in Washington."

When the waitress returned, Wayne ordered the crabs, then added, "What else, Stacy? Salad? A beer?"

"Both."

"That's it then. Crabs, salad and two beers."

Moments later, with newspapers spread over the table and paper bibs tied around their necks, they were smashing the shells of the crabs to get to the sweet, white meat, which they dipped in vinegar. They were so engrossed in eating that neither of them spoke. Wayne was frowning in concentration as he struggled with a chunk of crab still lodged in a claw. Stacy smiled as she watched him.

Catching her grin, he asked, "What's so amusing, Miss Allen?"

"You are, Congressman. Do you always concentrate so intensely on everything you do?"

Their eyes met across the table and in an instant her casual question took on a deeper meaning. Although her hand shook and her heart was beating rapidly, she was unable to look away. There was something so compelling, so intimate in that gaze that it left her breathless. The extended silence only heightened the anticipation she was feeling.

When Wayne spoke at last, his voice was low and husky with emotion. "Absolutely everything. For instance, right now I am finding it nearly impossible to think about anything but those huge, violet eyes of yours and that incredibly tempting mouth. If we weren't in the middle of a restaurant, I'd show you just how hard I could concentrate on those."

For a moment, Stacy couldn't bring herself to speak. She was afraid her voice would give her away, revealing how deeply his words had affected her. When she finally spoke, there was a note of warning in her voice.

"Congressman . . ."

"I know. I know," he said, throwing up his hands in mock surrender. "Any discussion of my attraction to you is off limits. I will try to refrain. However," he added with an infectious grin, "you make that a damn difficult assignment."

"But I'm sure you can handle it," Stacy said with feigned severity.

His sigh was exaggerated. "I'll try, if you insist."

"I insist," she said, suddenly looking up to find Pete Arnold standing by the table. She had no idea when he had walked over, but from the stern look on his face he'd apparently heard far too much of their conversation. Still, she managed a weak smile.

"Pete, what are you doing here?"

"Even news directors go out to dinner occasionally." Then, with a pointed look at Wayne, he added, "I see you're hard at work on your story."

She fought to keep a tone of defensiveness from her voice, as she said, "Yes. I am. You know the

Congressman, I'm sure. Congressman Dodge, this is my boss, Pete Arnold."

Wayne rose to shake his hand.

"It's a pleasure. I ought to thank you for sending Stacy to talk to me."

"Oh?" Pete said, his thick eyebrows lifting.

"She's a fine reporter. Very persistent."

Stacy flinched at Pete's look. "I'm glad to hear that," he said. "I hope she is also objective. I'll be looking forward to seeing the material she's gathered for this documentary."

His lack of subtlety was not lost on Stacy. Even Wayne should be able to sense the warning in those words.

Apparently feeling he had completed his duty, Pete excused himself. "Enjoy your dinner," he said, as he left to join his friends.

The uncomfortable encounter left Stacy with little appetite for the rest of her meal. After she'd sat in silence for some time, twisting her napkin into a knot with nervous fingers, Wayne sensed the full measure of her anxiety and called for the bill, so they could leave. However, they were crossing the bridge into Virginia before he brought up the subject of her withdrawal.

"Are you that upset about running into your boss?"

"You heard him," Stacy said flatly. "He suspects this was no business dinner."

"Why would he suspect that? Stacy, you're imagining things."

"No, I'm not."

"All right. So Pete Arnold doesn't think this was a business dinner. Suppose you're right about that? What difference can it possibly make?"

"You don't understand, do you? Our involvement could jeopardize my job, Wayne. How can I get that through your head?"

"Stacy, calm down," he said soothingly. We haven't done anything that could be remotely construed as wrong or even compromising."

"Not morally wrong. But there is a code of ethics in my profession. Reporters do not get emotionally involved with their subjects. It destroys their credibility, their objectivity, everything."

"Is that what's happened, then?" he asked gently. "Are you admitting that you are becoming emotionally involved with me?"

The question hung in the air between them. The tension it created was almost palpable.

"Yes," she whispered miserably, her voice ending on a soft cry. "Yes."

He pulled the car to the side of the road then and gathered her into his arms.

"Oh, Stacy, don't cry. This will all work out. I promise you. I want you more than anything."

At her muffled gasp, he held her more tightly, "Ssh, now. I won't push you. I won't ask for anything until after this documentary is over, if that's the way you want it. But when that time comes, you and I will have some serious things to discuss."

Stacy clung to him helplessly, lost in the overpowering sensations aroused by being in his arms, her face against the softness of his shirt, the musky masculine scent of him filling her with a desire to be even closer.

"In the meantime, though, it's all making my job impossible," she murmured against his chest.

"Give up the assignment then. There are other reporters."

"I can't. Pete is adamant about my doing it."

"Why?"

It was a perfectly reasonable question, but she knew she couldn't answer it, not without revealing far too much. She said only, "He has his reasons."

43

"And you're not going to tell me what they are?" he asked, a note of pain and weariness creeping into his voice.

"No," she said firmly. "I can't."

"Fine," he said coldly, drawing away from her. "You have repeatedly slammed the door in my face whenever the conversation takes a turn in some direction you want to avoid. That displays an incredible lack of trust in me."

Stacy blanched at his tone and the accuracy of his charge.

"Of course, there may be a reasonable explanation for your behavior. You may know that answers would destroy your chance of getting the story Pete wants so badly. Is that it, Stacy?"

When she didn't answer, he pushed even harder. "Is Pete Arnold using you to get me? Is he hoping to create some sort of scandal?"

Shock registered on Stacy's face, but before she could deny the accusation, he said flatly, "Because I assure you, Miss Allen, there will be no scandal."

"You can be sure of that, Congressman," she said in a voice filled with outrage.

"Hurts, doesn't it?" he said softly. "It hurts to be told by someone you respect that they think you're using them. That's what you did to me the other day, Stacy, when you accused me of trying to seduce you simply to influence the outcome of your damn documentary."

"You've made your point, Congressman," she said, covering her face with her hands, trying not to let him see her tears. "So, now we're even. What happens next?"

"This, I think," he suggested, pulling her gently back into his arms.

As his lips descended toward hers, her mouth opened in anticipation. His chin, rough with a day's growth of beard, scratched her tender skin, but the sensation was far from unpleasant. His mouth brushed lightly across hers, then tenderly kissed her cheeks, where tears had dampened them. When they returned to her mouth, his lips were met by her trembling ones in a hungry kiss. Her hand trailed along the side of his face, tenderly stroking his neck before coming to rest against his chest, where she could feel the rapid beat of his heart.

The tension of the kiss mounted, as his tongue teased her lips before finally penetrating to the soft inner sweetness. Stacy found herself responding in ways she never had before, daring to match the rising heat of his passion. Her body seemed to be wired in some peculiar way that allowed currents of electricity to sweep through her in exciting waves with each touch of Wayne's lips.

When he pulled back, she could see the intense, fiery longing she felt reflected in his eyes.

"Do you know how long I've wanted to do that?" he asked, cradling her against his side. "Ever since the first moment I saw you in that restaurant last week. You were so determined, so angry. I thought you were the most spirited, desirable woman I had ever seen."

Relaxing in his embrace, Stacy teased, "What about professional? Didn't you think I was very professional?"

"Very," he agreed with a wicked grin. "But, believe me, your professionalism was the last thought on my mind."

"Have I lived up to your expectations?" she demanded.

"Don't be coy, Miss Allen. It's not becoming. So far, though, yes. You've lived up to them quite nicely."

"So far?" she repeated breathlessly.

"So far," he echoed, as his hand drifted along the

suede of her jacket to rest on her breast. She shivered at the note of desire in his voice, as much as at his touch. When he reached inside the jacket, his stroke more insistent now, her nipple responded instantly.

He readjusted his position on the seat then and suddenly they were side by side, their bodies locked together in the cramped space. Hers, with a will of its own, strained toward his, wanting to feel more of its masculine hardness against her. As he shifted once more, his elbow hit the horn, sending out a sharp blast.

For an instant they lay still in each other's arms. Then, they both burst out laughing, as they struggled back to a sitting position from the tangle of arms, legs, and clothing they'd created.

"I am entirely too old to be doing this sort of thing in the front seat of a car," Wayne said with a sigh. "What have you done to me, Stacy Allen? I haven't done anything like this since I was eighteen."

"How boring for you," Stacy teased. "No wonder you're not married."

"Good Lord, you're impudent. I meant, my dear, that I've done nothing like this in a car. There are more satisfactory settings."

"So I've heard."

There was something in her voice, a hint of longing, perhaps, that made him look at her sharply.

"Are you saying what I think you're saying?" he asked, unable to keep the incredulity from his voice.

She shrugged, as though it didn't matter to her what he thought about her admission. "My Midwestern upbringing, I guess. I believed all that stuff about waiting for the right man."

He shook his head in wonder. "You're even more incredible than I thought. How did I ever manage to find you?"

"You didn't," she reminded him. "I found you."

"So you did."

"Still glad about it?" she asked shyly, her eyes downcast.

He cupped her chin and forced her to face him.

"More than ever," he said softly. "More than ever."

Five

The next morning Stacy couldn't keep her mind on anything except Wayne. She found herself lustily singing snatches of love songs as she drove to work. With each new tune, she remembered the way he'd looked at her when he'd kissed her good night. It had been a look filled with tenderness, a look that made her feel incredibly special and desirable.

Every now and then reality intruded on her sweet memories, reminding her that she faced a confrontation with Pete. But even that couldn't spoil the warm glow she was feeling.

She had been at her desk only a few minutes, when the phone rang.

"Stacy, Mr. Arnold wants to see you right away," his secretary said urgently. Then lowering her voice, she added, "I don't know what's going on, but he's being impossible this morning. You'd better get in here right away, hon."

"Thanks, Della. I'll be right there."

Stacy was filled with dread as she walked toward Pete's office. Through the window he'd had put in so he could look out over the newsroom, she saw that he was on the phone. Judging from his expression, it was not a pleasant conversation. Stacy paused by Della's desk. The older woman shook her head and whispered, "Good luck."

Stacy would have stayed safely by Della's side, but Pete saw her then and motioned for her to come in. Waving her toward a chair, he continued berating a reporter, who'd apparently missed making contact with a State Department spokesman who had issued a major policy statement.

"How the hell do you expect us to go on the air without film? This is television, not radio," he sarcastically reminded the reporter. "Go find the man and get him in front of a camera, even if you have to interrupt him in the john."

He slammed the phone back in its cradle, and Stacy winced as the desk rocked under the impact.

"As for you, young lady, I'd like an explanation," he demanded, barely pausing for breath after his tirade on the phone.

"An explanation about what?" Stacy asked, trying to buy time before he leveled the full force of his fury at her.

"You know exactly what," he said impatiently. "That cozy little dinner you were having with Wayne Dodge last night."

"It was for the story," she offered timidly.

"Like hell. If you got anything during dinner that you can put on the air, I will personally eat an entire reel of tape."

Stacy remained silent, staring at the floor.

"So? What did you get for the documentary?"

"All right," she said defensively. "I didn't get anything specific. But you told me you wanted me to be thorough, to get to know everything I could about

Dodge. How do you expect me to do that, if I don't spend time with him?"

"I can assure you I don't expect you to do it by sleeping with the man."

Furious, Stacy leapt to her feet and headed for the door. "I don't have to sit here for that sort of thing," she said coldly, her voice barely under control.

"Stacy!"

Pete's tone stopped her in her tracks.

"Get in here and sit down!" When she didn't move, he added, "Now!"

She returned to the chair, her hands clenched so tightly her knuckles were white.

Pete's voice was softer, as he told her, "I apologize for the remark. However, I want something clearly understood."

"What?" Stacy asked, meeting his eyes for the first time since the meeting had begun.

"If you and Wayne Dodge are about to become an item for the gossips in this town, I want to know about it now. From you. I don't want to read about it some morning in the *Style* section in the *Washington Post*. I'd hate to have my breakfast spoiled."

"Pete, I promise you there will be no gossip about me and the Congressman. I am doing a documentary about the man. That's where it starts and where it ends."

As she spoke, Stacy made herself a promise as well: She would see to it that what she was telling Pete was the truth, at least until after the documentary was completed and on the air. She would just have to make Wayne understand.

Pete was regarding her skeptically, but when he spoke he sounded convinced. "Fine. See that it stays that way."

Thus dismissed, Stacy started from the office. As she reached the door, Pete added one last question.

"By the way, Stacy, who paid for dinner last night?" Although his tone was casual, Stacy knew the question held all sorts of implications. She blushed with embarrassment.

"That's what I thought," he said, nodding. "See to it that you reimburse him. While you're on this assignment, you pay for the meals. I don't care how much that threatens his masculinity. Got it?"

"Yes, sir," she said, rushing from the office before he could think of anything else.

She certainly had botched everything up so far, she admitted to herself as she went back to her desk. She had done just about everything she could to compromise the integrity of her reporting. Well, she could still rectify things, if she was very careful from here on.

Her mouth twisted in an ironic grin, as she thought of the chemistry that seemed to ignite into an uncontrollable fire every time she and Wayne met. Could she fight that, she wondered.

Back at her desk she flipped through her messages, returning a couple of calls that seemed particularly urgent. She had just hung up from the last of these, when her phone rang.

"Stacy? How's my favorite public relations expert?" a booming voice asked.

"Jay? Is it really you? How are you?" Her voice was filled with delight. Suddenly she realized how much she'd missed Jay, since moving back to Washington. He'd been a good friend during those long months of the campaign, sort of like the big brother she'd never had. "Where are you?"

"Right here in town, as a matter of fact. Thought I'd take my favorite girl to lunch. Are you free?"

"To see you, always. Where should I meet you?"

He named a small, dimly lit restaurant only a couple of blocks from the Capitol. Unpretentious and frequented more by secretaries than power brokers, it was hardly the sort of place Jay usually liked.

"Why on earth would you want to go there?"

"Let's just say it's convenient," he said mysteriously.

"Convenient for what?"

"Never mind. Can you be there at one o'clock?"

"I'll be there," she agreed.

Fortunately she wouldn't have to wait long to solve the mystery. It was already after noon. By the time she freshened her make-up and caught a cab to the restaurant, it would be one o'clock. At the last minute, she stuck a notebook in her purse. The way Jay was behaving might mean there was a story involved. She'd better be prepared.

When she arrived at the cramped little sandwich shop, Jay was already there, seated at a table in an out-of-the-way corner. His early arrival and the table he'd chosen were out of character too. He usually loved the limelight, the best table, a late entrance. Stacy was more and more intrigued by his behavior.

Kissing him on the cheek, she sat across from him and demanded, "So, what's the big mystery? Why this place and all the cloak and dagger stuff?"

"You'll see," he said, patting her hand. "Be patient."

For several minutes he guided the conversation in a casual direction, asking about her job, her apartment, her friends. Stacy went along with his ploy, answering briefly and knowing absolutely that he didn't give a hoot about her replies.

"I hear you're doing a documentary about Wayne Dodge," he said at last.

Stacy nodded in sudden understanding. "So that's it? How did you find out?"

"Sweetie, nothing's a secret around this town for long. Are you doing the documentary or not?"

"You're the one with all the answers. You tell me."

"Stacy!"

"All right, yes. I am doing a show on Dodge. What about it?"

"I have a couple of little tidbits about the Congressman you might want to check out," he said, a smug look on his face.

"You're hardly an unbiased source, Jay. Do you plan to run against him again?"

"Probably, but what does that have to do with anything? The information's valid. You can check on it."

"Okay, since you're determined to tell me. What is it?"

"Did you know that he's been romancing the wife of a very prominent senator?"

Stacy's mouth dropped open in astonishment and she felt her heart sinking in dismay.

"Where . . . where did you hear that?" she asked reluctantly. "I know you don't like Wayne Dodge, Jay, but the man is not a fool. He wouldn't do something like that."

"Like I said, check it out. The way I hear it, though, the romance has been hot and heavy for months now. The only thing keeping the lid on is the fact that the husband needs Dodge to get a piece of legislation approved. Once he's accomplished that, he'll blow the whole thing open. It's going to be a nasty scandal."

Stacy thought of the time she'd spent with Wayne just yesterday, of the things he'd said to her. No, what Jay was saying couldn't be true.

"Sorry, Jay. I don't buy it," she said firmly.

"What will it take to convince you? Seeing them together?"

"That would be a start," she conceded.

"Then turn around and look over in the corner across the room. They just sat down."

Stacy didn't want to look. She didn't want to know about this. It had nothing to do with the story and everything to do with the way she felt about Wayne. Already her stomach was turning inside out. Maybe yesterday had been the lie, an attempt to use her publicly to distract attention from the affair he was having with a prominent, married woman.

With Jay watching her expectantly, waiting for her reaction, she had to turn around eventually. When she did, she spotted him instantly, his back to her as he leaned across the table toward his companion. At first Stacy's view of the woman was blocked, but when Wayne shifted slightly, her face became visible. Stunned, Stacy recognized her. It was the same lovely blonde who was with him the first night she met him.

There could be no doubt, then. She had seen them together twice now. Each time, she realized, the woman had been staring at him adoringly, her laughter echoing through the restaurant. That first night Stacy had taken hardly any note of the woman, but today she studied her intently. What she saw made her almost sick with despair.

She was clearly no match for this woman. She was obviously rich and pampered. The color and styling of her hair suggested she had regular beauty shop appointments at one of the finest salons. Her make-up was subtly flattering, designed to camouflage her age, which seemed to be in her mid-forties. She wore an expensive suit, a silk blouse, and shoes that Stacy recognized from an ad in a fashion magazine. Stacy was sure the shoes alone cost more than her weekly salary.

For one of the few times in her life, Stacy felt a real pang of envy. This woman had everything—beauty, wealth, even the love of a man whom Stacy admitted she wanted for herself. She found herself hating this woman, hating her with the irrational jealousy of a woman falling in love.

Jay remained silent while she observed the couple. Clearly he had no idea of the impact the scene was having. As ruthless as he could be, he would never have exposed her to this had he known that her interest in Wayne was anything other than professional. Stacy knew she had to find a way to extricate herself from this situation before she revealed her vulnerability.

As she turned back to him, she saw the triumphant gleam in his eyes and wanted to slap him. Instead, fighting to keep her voice steady, she asked, "Who is she?"

"Madeline Chase. Her husband is—"

"I know. Frederick Chase, ranking member of the House Foreign Relations Committee. But what makes you think his wife and Wayne Dodge are having an affair? Surely they'd be more discreet than this."

"You're the reporter, Stacy. All I know is what I hear around town and I've heard this often enough by now to be certain there's some truth to it."

Still struggling to deny what was right in front of her eyes, Stacy countered, "So what if it is true? In this day and age affairs are commonplace. Certainly this city is full of them. It doesn't make Dodge a bad Congressman."

Jay looked at her sharply.

"Why are you taking his side, Stacy? During the campaign you'd have given anything for a piece of information we could have used against Dodge. Now you're fighting it, as though you have some sort of personal stake in protecting him. Have you changed sides?"

"I'm not on anyone's side," she said, more sharply than she'd intended. "I'm a reporter trying to pull together an unbiased story about a politician. I'm not sure his sex life is the public's business."

"It is if it says something about his character," Jay retorted. "Isn't that what you used to say?"

"Yes, damn it. Don't push it, Jay. You've passed along your information. I'll check it out. If it seems relevant, I'll use it. Satisfied?"

"Hey," he said, throwing up his hands in surrender. "Don't snap my head off, but, yes, I'm satisfied."

"Then let's get out of here. I'm suddenly feeling sick to my stomach."

Back at the station, Stacy tried to work on the documentary, putting her notes into some sort of structure for the half-hour show. But by 4:30 P.M. she knew it was useless. She couldn't concentrate at all. Every piece of information created an image of Wayne and each of those images, in turn, brought Madeline Chase to her mind. It made every minute she worked a tiny torment.

Finally, she gave up. Sticking her head in the door to Pete's office, she said, "Unless you need me for something, I'm going home."

The note of dejection in her voice drew Pete's attention away from the pile of paperwork in front of him.

"Everything okay?" he asked, peering over the top of his bifocals.

"Sure. I've just hit some sort of stumbling block. I'm sure I'll be able to get back on the track by tomorrow."

"You sure that's all it is?"

She tried for a reassuring smile, but it was a weak one and didn't fool Pete for an instant. However, she insisted, "That's all. I'll be in here bright and early bursting with fresh ideas."

"Okay. See that you are. I want a progress report from you by tomorrow afternoon," he said sternly.

"You'll have it," she promised.

Normally Stacy hated the rush hour traffic, but today she was thankful to be in the midst of the bumper-to-bumper crush. It required total concentration, leaving her no time to conjure up more images of Wayne and Madeline Chase. The thought of him touching her, telling her he loved her, made Stacy's head throb. A cold, empty feeling seemed to have settled somewhere in her midsection and her eyes were burning with the tears she determinedly refused to shed.

At home she took a hot shower, hoping the pounding spray would soothe the muscles in her shoulders, easing the knots of tension. Rubbing herself briskly with a rough towel, her skin glowed. She pulled on a blue terrycloth robe, then fluffed her hair dry with a towel, creating a halo of dark curls to frame her pale face.

She wandered into the kitchen and poured herself a glass of chablis before settling down to watch the evening news. Paul Robbins had just started a follow-up report on little Becky, when the doorbell rang. Waiting to hear how the child was coming along, she was slow getting to the door. The bell buzzed again.

"Who is it?" she called.

"Wayne. Come on, Stacy, open the door."

Hearing his voice made whatever had frozen inside her begin to melt. She wanted him to come in and explain everything. Yet she knew he wouldn't, unless she asked and she couldn't do that.

As she stood there, immobilized by an assault of conflicting emotions, Wayne hollered impatiently, "Stacy, what's wrong? Are you planning to keep me standing out here all night? Let me in, damn it. There's something you and I need to discuss. Now!"

The arrogance of his attitude suddenly infuriated Stacy. What in heaven's name did he have to be angry or upset about? She was the one who had been duped and here he was behaving as though he'd been wronged.

She opened the door and faced him defiantly. "What are you doing here?"

"I told you. We have some things to talk about," he said and moved past her.

She closed the door and followed him into the room, where he was pacing, his hands clenched at his sides. In amazement, she realized he really was furious. He paused in his pacing to pick up her wine glass and take a taste.

"Any more of this?" he asked.

"In the kitchen. I'll get you a glass."

"Never mind," he said sharply. "I'll find it. You just sit down."

Suddenly Stacy exploded. The tension of the afternoon, seeing him with a married woman with whom he was apparently having a well-known fling, his attitude now, it was all more than she could stand.

"Who the hell do you think you are, Congressman?" she shouted, halting him immediately. Stunned by her outrage, he faced her as she continued. "You have no right to come in here unannounced, no right to yell at me and issue orders. This is my home, Congressman. From now on you'll come here on invitation only and you'll behave like a gentleman. As for tonight, I think you'd better get out, because I'm in no mood for you and this temper you seem to be in."

"You're not in the mood," he said incredulously. "Listen, kiddo, I'm not exactly boiling over with delight at the way this day has gone myself, thanks to you. But I decided to be fair, to come over here and give you a chance to explain."

"Give me a chance to explain?" Stacy's laugh was bitter. "Explain what? If anyone around here ought to do some explaining, it's you."

Wearily, Wayne held up his hands. "Okay. Okay. Look, it's clear there have been some misunderstandings. Would you please just sit down for a minute and let me get a glass of wine? When I get back, maybe we can straighten all this out."

Stacy faced him belligerently, her hands on her hips.

"Sit down, Stacy!" he said sternly, then added more gently, "please."

She sat down, watching him warily as he moved about the kitchen looking for a glass and the rest of the wine.

When he came back into the living room, he sank dejectedly into the chair across from her, his shoulders hunched forward. He took a sip of his wine, then held the glass up toward the light, studying it as though somehow it might hold the key to unlocking the mystery of why this day had been so miserable.

When he spoke at last, his voice was flat, devoid of emotion. "How do you know J.J. Lawrence?"

Stacy's head jerked up at the question, but seeing the look of pain on his face, she looked away. So, she thought, that was it. He had seen her at the restaurant with Jay. No wonder he was so angry. He'd felt as betrayed as she had seeing him with Madeline Chase.

"Stacy, answer me," he insisted. "How do you know him? Are you interviewing him for the documentary?"

For a fleeting moment she thought of saying yes, letting him believe that Jay was just another source for the show. It would be an easy solution and it would only be a small lie. After all, Jay had given her some information, though right now she was damning him for it.

Stacy couldn't bring herself to say the words. No matter how small, it would only be another lie between them and there had already been far too many lies.

"No," she said softly. "I wasn't interviewing him."

"What then?"

She took a deep breath, knowing that what she was about to say could spoil everything.

"I used to work for Jay," she admitted slowly.

Stunned disbelief replaced the look of pain and weariness on Wayne's face.

"You what?" he shouted. "You worked for Jay Lawrence? When?"

"In California," she said reluctantly, watching the shock seem to seep through him, draining him of his energy and his spirit. "I handled his public relations in his campaign against you."

She blurted the last out quickly. It was in the open now. The whole truth. But she couldn't bear to look at him to see how he was taking it. Suddenly an embittered, chilling laugh filled the room.

"My God, what an absolute fool I've been," he murmured softly, studying her with contempt. "I never had a prayer with this documentary, did I? You've been out to destroy me from the start."

"No," she denied, hating the way he was looking at her. "Please, Wayne, you can't believe that. I'm a reporter. My work for Jay was over months ago. It has nothing to do with this."

"How can you say that? You spent what, six months, a year, campaigning for my opponent and you're trying to tell me that doesn't influence what you're doing now?"

"It doesn't. I swear to you, it doesn't."

"Stacy, I'm not naive. I heard J.J. Lawrence's speeches. I debated the man. You handled his public relations, so you must have written a great deal of his material. Are you trying to tell me you didn't believe what you were writing?"

The tears that had been threatening all day overflowed now and Stacy was powerless to stop them. They slid silently down her cheeks, as she tried to think of the words that would make him understand. How could she explain, make him see that was another time, another place, a lifetime ago?

"I believed it at the time," she said haltingly. "I . . . I don't anymore."

"Really?" he said sarcastically. "What sudden revelation changed your mind?"

"You did. I've gotten to know you."

"Too bad you're not still in California. A converted voter is always nice to have." He lifted his glass to her in a mocking toast.

"Don't make jokes, Wayne. Please," she begged. "I'm telling you the truth. I still . . . still don't agree with everything you say, with all of your stands, but I've never doubted your integrity. Not even back then. Couldn't you tell that from Jay's speeches? They were never attacks on you, only on your positions."

"Honey, I am my positions. That's what politics is all about. It's when you stop believing in the positions you take that the trouble begins. Then you can be bought by just about anyone. Surely you've noticed that about your friend Lawrence. He rarely takes the same stand on an issue twice. It's usually whatever's the most expedient."

Stacy had no answer for that. Wayne was right. No matter how much she might wish it were otherwise, her speeches for Jay had been attacks on Wayne. He could not be separated from his position on immigration or on the Middle East, any more than she could be separated from the stories she did. If her name was on them, they were hers to stand behind, to defend. Why else had she fought so hard to insist that each detail be accurate, that there be no twisting of facts to achieve a more dramatic story? Like Wayne, all she had going for her in her profession was her integrity.

Now, though, she had to convince Wayne to trust her again, to believe that her integrity was of paramount importance to her and that the documentary would be impartial as a result.

"Wayne, you've got to believe me. None of this matters anymore. The documentary will be fair. That's why Pete wanted me to do it, you know. Remember I told you he'd insisted on it. He said it was because he knew I'd bend over backward to be unbiased. And I will. I promise."

Slowly Wayne got to his feet and stood towering over her. The look on his face was murderous.

"I don't believe this! You actually intend to go through with this . . . this farce?"

Stacy flinched in the face of his fury, but she didn't hesitate for a moment. "Of course. I have no choice. It's my assignment and Pete's not about to take me off of it."

"Well, you won't be doing it with my cooperation any longer," he said angrily. "Nor will anyone on my staff cooperate."

"Don't be foolish," she begged. "If you don't cooperate, how can I possibly present an unbiased picture of you? Don't you see? I need your help to do that."

"You need my help to get you off the hook," he sneered cynically. "Without my participation your documentary won't carry any weight at all, especially not after people in this town find out about your background. They'll assume it was a hatchet job. That won't help your reputation in the media much, will it?"

"No," she admitted, her voice filled with resignation. "It will probably mean the end of my career . . . in Washington, anyway. But," she said, trying to inject some spirit into her voice, "I'll find work someplace. I'm a damn good reporter, Congressman, whatever you may think of me. I'm just not a very lucky one. I managed to pull the one story that could nearly destroy my career. If that's the way you want it, be my guest. I'll do my damnedest to do a thorough documentary about you and then you can spread the word and destroy me. I'd say that's quite a deal for both of us."

Without looking up, she took a long, slow drink of her wine. When she heard him leave, the door closing softly behind him, she put the glass on the table, her hand shaking.

Six

Long after Wayne had left, Stacy remained in the same position, staring into the darkness. She made no move to turn on the lights, nor was she even aware of the television's soft murmur in the background. The news had ended long ago and in its place a smiling game show host mocked her mood with his theatrical enthusiasm.

Her nerves felt raw, as though they had sought love and comfort and instead had come up against something harsh, unyielding and painful. Her spirits fluctuated in a wild swing between fury at Wayne's obstinate refusal to see her point of view and an incredible loneliness at the realization that he had walked out of her life for good. In the long run, it was the latter that was far more devastating.

There were ways she could do the story without his cooperation. It wouldn't be as complete, as three-dimensional, but it would make its point. Viewers might not even be aware that he had declined to appear in front of her camera, if file film of him was edited into the finished documentary in a judicious way.

However, it wouldn't be nearly as simple to replace his presence in her personal life. In such a short time he had taken over her heart and her mind, challenging her in ways that were entirely new and exciting. It had been the most stimulating period in her life.

Now, suddenly, she was bereft. There was no one with whom she could exchange the ideas that were dancing around in her head. Nor was there anyone she could talk to about her feelings. Pete certainly wouldn't understand. Even Paul was out of the question. Both had warned her against this involvement.

She longed for a close friend to share her heartache, but the few women she had known well in Washington during her college days were gone now. Her childhood friend, Amanda, would listen, but in the years since her marriage and the birth of her first baby, she had seemed remote somehow, as though she could no longer fully understand Stacy's lifestyle or her problems.

So, there was no one. She would have to muddle through this alone. Ironically tonight's confrontation had overshadowed another problem—Wayne's alleged romance with Madeline Chase. She'd almost forgotten about it.

Sighing, she said aloud, "Oh, well. What does it matter now?"

Certainly it shouldn't matter. Not to the documentary and not to her. But, if she were to be totally honest, it mattered dreadfully. She didn't want to believe, even now, that the man who'd said he loved her was already involved with another woman. An older, married woman at that!

Her thoughts whirled, filled with images of Wayne and Madeline Chase on the two occasions she had seen them together. They certainly looked as though they were close, now that she thought about it. There was an implied intimacy in the way she had touched him as they talked and in her possessive glances at him.

"Damn, it's over! Forget it," she swore softly, knowing that it was a futile cry. Exhausted by the night's events and no longer able to deal with the pain they had caused, she dragged herself to bed. Although it was barely nine o'clock, perhaps she could escape into sleep, blotting out the anguish until morning. Perhaps then she could find a way to cope.

But a night filled with troubling dreams made her sleep restless and she awoke emotionally and physically drained. A cool shower did little to revive her, but sheer determination drove her to finish getting ready for work. A cup of coffee improved her alertness, if not her spirits, and by eight o'clock she was on her way to the station.

At her desk she found a stack of messages, including several from Jay marked urgent. Nothing he could possibly have to say was that important, she decided, tossing the messages aside. She would deal with him later. She wasn't up to any more of his revelations this morning.

She got a steaming cup of black coffee and brought it back to her desk, forcing herself to go through her notes and begin planning the documentary. She'd need to rough out a basic script and a shooting schedule before her meeting with Pete this afternoon. He'd want to know exactly what she had planned before he okayed the use of a film crew and set a tentative airdate.

One issue had surfaced again and again during her research and she finally settled on it as the focus for the half-hour show. Wayne was becoming closely identified with the fight to stop the tide of illegal immigrants from Mexico and to prevent their exploitation by factory owners in California. There would be plenty of file footage of his public statements on the subject and a California station might be able to provide some special location film. Pete might even okay a trip to Los Angeles so she could take a close look at some of these sweat shops for herself. With the right film, this would be quite a show, she thought, but there was no feeling of satisfaction in the thought.

She was typing her script outline, when the phone rang.

"Stacy Allen," she answered.

"Stacy, it's Jay. Didn't you get my messages?"

"I got them."

"Then why didn't you call me back?"

"I've been busy, Jay," she said wearily. "What's so urgent?"

"I've been invited to a party. Thought you might like to come along."

"Jay, I'm in no mood for a party. Thanks, anyway."

"You might be in the mood for this one. The Chases are giving it. Tonight. What about it?"

Stacy was taken aback. "The Chases. Who invited you?"

"That's not very flattering," Jay said petulantly. "I do have some political pull in this town, even though I lost the election."

"Jay, I'm sorry. I didn't mean to be rude. I'm just surprised. I didn't know you knew the senator and his wife."

"I don't," he admitted. "But I have friends who do and they've invited me to bring a guest and meet them there. Come on, Stacy, you remember how much fun we had at all those campaign parties. Come with me. Besides, there might be a story in it for you."

Stacy had no doubt what story he meant and it

was the last one she wanted to pursue. An evening with Madeline Chase would be more than she could bear right now.

Still, Jay was right about one thing: It would be a chance to see firsthand the way Washington's social scene was ruled by politics. An awful lot of official and unofficial business was conducted at these affairs and even more of it found its way into print and on the air as a result. No one yet had found a way to stop the casual leaks that occurred at such parties.

"Okay, Jay," she said at last. "I'll go with you."

Her reluctance must have been plain, even to someone as insensitive as Jay. Indeed, he said, "Hey, don't put yourself out on my account, Stacy. I just thought you'd enjoy it."

"I'm sorry. I'm sure it will be fun. What time should I be ready?"

"Cocktails are at 7:30 P.M. I'll pick you up about seven. Tell me how to get to your place."

She gave him directions, then went back to her outline, putting the party from her mind. She spent the rest of the morning polishing up the idea, so she was ready for Pete when he called her into his office after lunch.

"How's it going?" he asked, eyeing her with concern.

"I think the show's going to be terrific."

"Actually, I was wondering more about you. You look beat."

"Thanks," she said sarcastically.

"Okay. So you're not beat and there's nothing wrong. I'll drop the subject. Tell me about the show."

She outlined her plan quickly, managing to avoid the fact that Wayne wasn't participating directly. When she suggested making a trip to Los Angeles, he agreed readily.

"Call out there and arrange for a crew to work

with you for a couple of days, then have Della make your travel arrangements. How soon do you think you can pull this together?"

"With any luck, three to four weeks. If we've got breathing room, I'd rather have six. I want this to be really good."

Pete looked at her sharply, but apparently decided to let the comment pass without cross-examining her about why she felt so strongly about this particular production all of a sudden.

"Okay, kid, get going on it and keep me posted. I won't put it in the schedule until you finish the shooting and know what you have. How's that?"

"Great."

Stacy filled the rest of the afternoon with travel plans, arranging for a film crew and getting Della to confirm her reservations. She could fly out over the weekend, spend Monday and Tuesday with the crew and be back in the office on Wednesday. That would keep her right on schedule. It would also allow her a brief break over the weekend to visit with some old friends. The thought of that cheered her.

She tried to recapture that mood at home, as she rummaged through her closet for something to wear to the party. Nothing seemed quite right to her critical eye and she tossed aside one outfit after another until her bed was covered with a colorful, crazyquilt assortment of clothes. Finally, disgusted with her inability to make a decision and realizing that she was running out of time, she went back to a purple tube top covered with sequins, a sheer overblouse with a plunging neckline and long sleeves and a pair of matching silk evening pants.

She turned slowly in front of the mirror. With her long, shapely legs, full breasts, pale complexion and violet eyes, it was a stunning look. It might give her the courage she'd need to get through this meeting with Madeline Chase and her husband.

She took extra care with her make-up, then put on the purple and silver headband that always made her feel as if she'd just stepped out of the pages of *Vogue* or *Glamour*. The whole effect was a little daring and very contemporary, a far cry from the sedate wardrobe she wore at work. When the doorbell rang, she gave herself a wink of encouragement before going to meet Jay.

The time she'd spent getting ready had apparently been worth every second. Jay appeared dumfounded for several minutes, then his eyes lit with appreciation.

"My God, Stacy. You look spectacular!"

She grinned. "Not the Stacy Allen you're used to, is it?"

"Hardly, but I love it. You'll knock 'em dead. I just hope the Senator's ready for you. I've heard he has a heart condition."

"Thanks for thinking I'm devastating, love, but I doubt I'll affect the man's health."

Jay shook his head dazedly. "I don't know. My heart's beating erratically."

"Well, get it under control, old friend. This isn't meant to turn you on."

Suddenly turning serious, he asked, "Who is it meant for, Stacy? Wayne Dodge?"

Now it was Stacy's turn to be astounded. Defensively she asked, "Why on earth would you ask a crazy question like that? Surely Wayne Dodge won't even be at this party."

"I suspect he'll be very much in evidence," Jay contradicted. "Remember what I told you. The Senator needs his vote."

Jay's comment silenced her. Had she known deep down inside that Wayne would be there tonight?

Was that why her appearance had been so important to her? No. It couldn't be, she thought. She had only wanted to look her best, because these were important people and because Madeline Chase was the hostess. Wayne had had nothing to do with it. In fact, if she'd known he might be there, would she even have agreed to go? Probably not.

Well, it was too late now to back out. In fact, Jay was repeating impatiently, "Stacy, are you ready?"

"Sure," she said slowly, picking up her silver purse and taking a deep breath as she followed him to the door.

The drive to Georgetown went quickly. Too quickly it seemed to Stacy, whose stomach seemed to be filled with a chorus line of tiny tap dancers. Several other couples were also arriving, as they walked up the cobbled path to the impressive brick townhouse. Stacy recognized two Congressmen, a high-level Cabinet official, and a network newsman. If this group of arrivals was typical, there was going to be quite a turnout.

Just inside the door, they were greeted by Senator Chase and his wife. The Senator looked fit, despite his recent heart attack, and he greeted Jay as though they were old friends.

"I've heard a great deal about you, young man. I hope we haven't seen the last of you in politics."

"I hope not too, Senator."

The older man, his face tanned and his handshake firm, smiled warmly at Stacy. "And who is this lovely young lady?" he asked Jay.

"Stacy Allen, Senator."

"Welcome, both of you. Now I'd like you to meet my wife," he said, drawing her closer to his side.

Stacy and Madeline Chase exchanged cautious glances. The older woman, her blond hair swept back from her face in a flattering style, looked regal beside her rugged, portly husband. Her skin had a soft, pearly glow that allowed her to get away with the black gown she was wearing. She smiled at Stacy, but the smile never reached her eyes and her grasp, when she shook hands, was weak and cool.

"Welcome, my dear," she said in a melodic voice that oddly held no note of warmth.

Stacy realized that Madeline Chase had recognized her. She also read in her eyes another message that was far more startling. This woman hated her! The intensity of her dislike was like a volt of current that cut right through Stacy. Fortunately there were others waiting to meet the hostess, allowing Stacy to escape from the cold hatred in those eyes.

If Jay had noticed anything out of the ordinary about her encounter with Madeline Chase, he said nothing about it. He was far too anxious to get into the living room, where he could mingle and begin building support for his next campaign. Jay never missed an opportunity to make powerful friends. For the rest of the evening he would expect her to fend for herself. She had done it often enough in California and, since she and Jay had never had a personal relationship, she wasn't bothered by the arrangement. It allowed her to stand back and observe.

Long ago she'd found that the intricate choreography at this sort of party was fascinating to watch. People came together, touched—a fleeting kiss on the cheek, a polite exchange of pleasantries—then moved on, always seeking someone more powerful.

Stacy accepted a glass of wine from a passing waiter and was about to move on, when she felt someone lay a cool hand on her arm.

"Miss Allen." The voice was chilly and commanding. Stacy turned to find Madeline Chase at her side.

Although her stomach was fluttering nervously, she managed a polite comment.

"It's a lovely party, Mrs. Chase."

"Let's skip the pleasantries, shall we, Miss Allen," the woman said with an icy disdain. "You and I need to talk. Would you come with me please?"

Stacy could see no way to refuse without creating a scene. Besides, perversely, she wanted to know what made this woman tick and what she could possibly have to say to her. She followed her to a small terrace that was deserted, now that the air was growing cool.

"I'm sure you know what I want to discuss with you," Mrs. Chase began.

"Actually, I don't. Why don't you enlighten me?"

"I want you to stay away from Wayne Dodge," she said in a low voice that hissed with anger.

Nothing she could possibly have said would have shocked Stacy more.

"I beg your pardon?"

"Don't play dumb, Miss Allen. You're a bright enough lady to follow me. Stay away from Wayne."

"Mrs. Chase, I am doing a documentary about the Congressman, as I am sure you are aware. That may necessitate my seeing him. If it does, all your threats won't keep me away from him."

"I don't give a damn about your documentary, although I understand he has no intention of cooperating with you on that."

Stacy's startled expression confirmed what she had only been guessing. "I see I'm right. But, as I said, Miss Allen, your documentary doesn't interest me. However, if you have some notion of starting a, shall we say, more personal relationship with Wayne, get it out of your head. He's mine. Do I make myself clear?"

Her voice was cold as ice, her expression formidable.

Stacy wasn't about to start a fight with her in her own home. What would be the point, anyway? She had no hold on Wayne, so why argue about it? Madeline Chase was determined to have her way in this and Stacy saw no logical reason not to let her.

Still, the woman's words, confirming her worst fears about her relationship with Wayne, tore at Stacy's heart. She wanted desperately to be left alone, to suffer privately the humiliation she was feeling. Fortunately, Madeline Chase apparently had said all she wanted to say. Without another word, she went back into the house, satisfied she had accomplished what she had set out to do.

Stacy was left alone on the terrace, tears stinging her eyes. "So, it's true," she thought miserably. "Everything Jay said is true."

Chilled by the facts she could no longer ignore, as much as by the night air, she shivered uncontrollably. Suddenly, she felt a jacket being draped over her shoulders.

"Want to talk about it?" the familiar, deep voice asked with surprising gentleness.

Looking up, she found Wayne beside her, puffing nervously on a cigarette, as he stared off into the distance.

"No," she said in a tight, choked voice.

He shrugged. "That's par for the course."

Unable to respond, Stacy felt the silence between them grow increasingly uncomfortable. The mounting tension was almost unbearable.

Still not looking at her, he broke the silence to ask, "What are you doing here?"

"I came with . . . someone," she said haltingly, unwilling to admit that Jay had brought her.

"Jay Lawrence, I suppose," he said and viciously stubbed out the cigarette, then tossed the butt over the rail of the balcony.

Sighing softly, she admitted it. "Yes. But it's not what you think."

"What does it matter what I think? It's your life."

"It matters to me," she said, her voice trembling. "Wayne, please. Can't we talk about this, start over? Everything's gotten so mixed up."

"Have we got anything left to work out, Stacy?" he asked doubtfully.

Trembling with trepidation, she took a step closer to him.

"This," she said quietly, leaning forward to kiss him, a fleeting touch of their lips that instantly revived all of the potent sensations he was capable of arousing in her. She stepped back then, waiting to see what response her daring gesture would bring.

For a moment Wayne did nothing. He stood stiff and still, as he faced her, his eyes focused on some distant point over her head. Then with a sudden groan, his body shuddering, he took her in his arms and held her tightly. Crushed against the broad expanse of his chest, Stacy felt herself go weak. Then Wayne was kissing her, one hand on her waist to hold her molded against his body. At that contact, it was as though a tiny match had been struck, igniting a fire that raged through their bodies. Their skin burned to the touch. Stacy could feel that Wayne's response matched her own, as his heart pounded and his hardened muscles trembled with a tension held tightly under control.

His lips left hers and traveled lightly along the hot, bare skin of her neck and chest. A hand slipped inside the tube top to fondle her already sensitive breast and a warmth began radiating from within, heating rapidly to match the white hot sensation his touch caused to her skin.

Stacy's head was thrown back, her lips parted on a sigh of pure erotic pleasure. She was lost to the sensations stirred by his unrelenting touch, which had drifted lower now to skim tantalizingly over the silk of her evening pants in a way that aroused her to new heights of joy.

Breathless, longing for fulfillment, she gasped, "Please, Wayne. Please, couldn't we leave here?"

Suddenly she was cast aside, the tight band of his arms no longer embracing her. When her puzzled glance met his eyes, she saw something cruel and mocking in them.

"Whatever would your date say, Miss Allen?" The cold sarcasm in his voice made her tremble with an unexplained fear.

"Jay?" she asked weakly. "What has Jay got to do with any of this?"

"Perhaps that's the question I should be asking. What does Jay Lawrence have to do with this sudden surge of passion? Are you still scheming with him in some twisted way to get me?"

Stacy was stunned by the cold fury in his voice. The charge was absurd. Couldn't he see that she was in love with him? Or didn't he care? Well, damn him either way, she thought bitterly.

"You really are despicable," she lashed out at him. "You wouldn't know an honest emotion, if it came up and introduced itself. Do you enjoy playing these little love scenes with me and then running back to your married mistress? Do the two of you have a good laugh over it? Well, Congressman, it's really over now. I'm bowing out as your sideshow. You can find someone else to substitute, when your ladyfriend is stuck at home with her husband."

She tore past him then, stumbling blindly past the startled guests, trying frantically to find the front door so she could escape from this place that seemed to have turned into a carnival house of horrors. It was a house filled with twisted minds and distorted faces.

She didn't hear Wayne call out to her. Nor was she aware that he had been prevented from following her by Madeline Chase, who had blocked his path.

Outside, Stacy had no trouble locating a taxi. She jumped into the back seat and gave the driver her address, knowing how much these Washington taxi drivers hated making the trip into Virginia. Fortunately, he didn't refuse to take her. She wasn't sure she could have held herself together long enough to find another cab.

On the ride home, which seemed so much longer now than it had earlier in the evening, she fought to bring her tears under control. The one tissue she'd put in her tiny purse was useless now, already damp from too many tears. Silently the taxi driver stuck his hand over the seat with a clump of clean tissues.

"Thanks," Stacy said shakily.

"Fight with your boyfriend?" he asked kindly.

"Something like that."

"You young people," he said, shaking his head. "Least sign of trouble, you run away. In my generation we were taught to stick around and work things out. Nowadays, you go home to momma or your psychiatrist or straight to a divorce lawyer. It's crazy. Those folks can't give you the answers you need."

"I know that," Stacy said, sniffling. "But in this situation there are no answers."

"Humph!" he snorted derisively. "There are always answers, young lady. Sometimes you just don't want to hear them."

"Maybe so," Stacy agreed, hoping to end the lecture. It reminded her of something her father might have said if he were alive. That thought made her sad and threatened to bring on a new flood of tears.

The driver seemed to understand her need to absorb his comments and he remained silent until he pulled up in front of her building. Then he added a last piece of advice.

"You listen to me, miss," he said sternly. "You call that young man of yours and tell him you want to talk this all out. Don't let some crazy, false pride stand in your way. If he's the man you love, fight for him."

Stacy grinned weakly.

"Maybe you should have been a psychiatrist yourself."

"What?" he said in mock horror. "And deal with the same crazy people week after week? Never. This way I get a new one every few minutes."

"But don't you ever wonder how things turned out?"

"Once in a while," he admitted with a smile. "But this way I get only happy endings. Night, young lady. You remember what I told you."

"I will," Stacy promised.

Upstairs, she discarded her stylish outfit and put on a nightgown and robe. Too restless to sleep, she got a glass of wine and settled down in her favorite corner of the sofa. She was barely seated when the phone and the doorbell rang simultaneously.

Answering the phone first, she heard Wayne's voice, still flat and cold. "Stacy?"

"Yes. Can you hold on just a second? There's someone at the door."

She ran across the room and called through the door.

"Who is it?"

"Me. Jay."

She opened the door.

"Come on in. I'll be right with you."

Picking up the phone again, she apologized. "Sorry."

"I just wanted to be sure you got home safely," he said stiffly.

"As you can see, I did," she said, matching his tone. "Anything else?"

He seemed about to say something, then apparently changed his mind. The silence extended over several more minutes.

Finally he asked, "Is that Lawrence there now?"

"Yes."

"I see."

Wearily, she pleaded, "Please, let's not start that again."

"Okay. You're right. It'll just lead to another argument. Stacy," he continued, his voice suddenly hesitant. "Look, I know this isn't the time, but could we talk?"

"I wanted to talk tonight," she reminded him.

"Oh?" he said, his tone lightly teasing. "Is that what you wanted? I had the impression you wanted something else entirely."

Chagrined by the accuracy of his remark, she said, "With us one thing usually leads to another."

"Yes, it does," he conceded with a laugh, though there was nothing particularly happy about the sound. "But what I want to do now is talk. Really talk. Can we do that?"

"Certainly."

"When?"

"Anytime you say, Congressman. It's your interview."

"Please, don't mention that word to me right now. It muddies up the picture."

"Sorry."

"And, dammit, stop apologizing," he exploded. "We're behaving like a couple of ridiculous schoolchildren. Stacy, I thought we had something promising going between us. Can't we get it back?"

"I told you, Congressman, anytime you say."

"Tomorrow? Dinner?"

"Fine."

"How about my place? We won't be interrupted there."

"All right. I should be able to get over there by seven thirty. Is that okay?"

"Perfect. I'll see you then. Oh and one more thing, I'm sorry about tonight," he said softly, hanging up before she could reply.

Stacy had no time to wonder about this latest turn of events. Jay was pacing around the room like a man possessed.

"Can I get you a glass of wine?" she offered.

Without answering her, he faced her and exploded, "What the hell happened over there tonight? I was in the middle of a conversation with a couple of senators and Madeline Chase came running up to tell me you'd gone flying out the door in hysterics. She insisted that I follow you."

"That certainly must have spoiled your evening," Stacy suggested without the slightest twinge of regret.

"As a matter of fact, it did," Jay said, his voice sounding like that of a spoiled child.

"Look, Jay, I'm sorry if I ruined your evening. There was no need for you to come running after me. We have been to enough of these functions together to know that once we're there, we're on our own. I don't require your protection, your attention or your escort services. You were certainly free to stay and finish your conversation."

"Not with Madeline Chase practically pushing me out the front door. I couldn't imagine why she'd be so concerned over someone she'd barely met unless you were really in bad shape."

Stacy found the idea of Madeline's concern laughable, but to Jay she said only, "I'm sure she was just being a polite hostess."

"Maybe so. But why did you leave in such a rush?"

"It was nothing. I just had a discussion with someone and things got a little awkward after that. I decided to leave."

"Your discussion wasn't by any chance with the Congressman?"

"What if it was? What difference could it possibly make to you?"

"None . . . to me. But if it's the Congressman you're investigating, a lot of other people may think otherwise. Stacy, despite all the garbage I give you from time to time, I do care about you. Stay away from Wayne Dodge. At least until after you finish this documentary."

Stacy sighed deeply. "Not you, too."

"I take it I'm not the first to offer this advice."

"In some cases it's been more like a warning."

"Whatever it is, the point is valid and you know it."

"When did you turn moralist?"

Jay grinned at her impudently. "Just a little of your own medicine. Remember what you told me every time I felt inclined to chase after some of the cute reporters during the campaign?"

"I'm sorry I ever opened my mouth," she said ruefully.

"You shouldn't be. It was good advice then and it's good now. Wayne Dodge may not give a damn about what this does to your career, but you certainly should. You've worked hard to get this job. Don't blow it over some . . . some stupid infatuation."

"Is that what you think this is all about—a stupid infatuation?"

"Isn't it?"

When Stacy couldn't bring herself to meet his gaze,

he whistled softly. "Good grief, kid. You aren't in love with the man, are you?"

"Don't sound so horrified."

"How do you expect me to sound? The man is trouble for you. To top it off, he's already involved with a married woman. You're going to get hurt, Stacy."

"Probably," she admitted.

"But you're not going to back away while there's still time?" he said incredulously.

Her laugh was harsh. "Time's already run out, Jay. Despite everything I promised myself and some other people, I'm in this thing way over my head."

Jay came and sat beside her, placing a comforting arm around her shoulders.

"Okay, kid. It's your life. If there's anything I can ever do to help, I'll be around."

"Thanks, Jay. I know you must feel as though I'm going over to the enemy."

"Honey, in this business, there are only political enemies. It's nothing personal. Under other circumstances, I might even like Wayne Dodge. He's not a bad man."

"So," she said triumphantly. "You admit it."

Jay had started for the door, but now he turned back to her. "Sure, I admit it . . . to you. But I still intend to beat him next time around."

He winked at her, then added, "Good luck, tiger."

Stacy smiled, as he shut the door. Tiger? She felt more like a weak kitten. How on earth was she going to get through the next few weeks?

Seven

A heightened sense of awareness seemed to be with Stacy all through the next day. She was anticipating this dinner with Wayne with an almost breathless nervousness. As eager as she was to see him, to resolve their differences, she feared what might happen next.

Trying to analyze the emotions warring within her, she realized that her conscience was battling her heart and, although she knew her heart would win in the end, she was hoping her conscience could postpone the inevitable for a little while longer. Nothing would happen with Wayne unless she wanted it to, unless she allowed it, she reminded herself repeatedly. And she had no intention of allowing anything. She was worried about her career, too. She should have herself taken off this assignment!

"Famous last words," she murmured softly to herself, giving a rueful grin to her reflection in the mirror of the station lounge.

Stacy slipped out of her tailored suit and into a silk dress in a deep shade of blue. The soft material skimmed over her figure, revealing the alluring curves.

A combination of guilt and uneasiness stayed with her during the drive to Wayne's place. When she arrived, she avoided the parking place directly in front of the townhouse and parked around the corner, then chided herself for behaving like a fool.

At the front door, her earlier excitement began replacing the other emotions. She rang the bell and waited expectantly. When no one answered, she rang again. Suddenly all the excitement and anticipation drained from her, replaced by a tiny knot of pain.

"What kind of game is he playing now?" she muttered, as she started toward her car. Just as she reached the sidewalk, she saw his sports car racing down the block. Its tires squealed in protest as he turned sharply into the driveway.

"Thank heavens, you hadn't left yet," he said, as he climbed out of the car and reached into the back for a bag of groceries. "Sorry I'm late, but I'd forgotten that I'd given the housekeeper the night off and promised her I'd take care of the shopping for our dinner."

"My, my, Congressman. This is a whole new side of your character," Stacy teased. "I'd never thought of you as disorganized before."

"I'm not usually," he said, bending to kiss the tip of her nose. "It seems to have come on quite recently."

The look in his eyes made her heart beat more rapidly, but she said impudently, "Perhaps you should be checked by a doctor. I've heard one of the first signs of senility is a lapse of memory."

"Miss Allen, my memory hasn't lapsed one bit. It's simply occupied with more pleasant images than groceries these days. Now help me get these things in the house or we won't be having dinner until midnight."

"I've heard midnight suppers are very romantic," she said softly.

"They are," he agreed, putting the groceries down on the kitchen counter. "But I'm in a rush tonight."

"Oh," Stacy said flatly, her high hopes for the evening suddenly deflating.

Wayne caught the expression on her face. "Hey, I'm not trying to get rid of you," he reassured her. "I'm only in a hurry to finish dinner . . . so we can get on to something more interesting."

A burning heat spread over Stacy's body at the sensuous gleam in his eyes, as they roamed slowly and possessively over her. The unexpected force of her desire left her weak, but she had no time to indulge in the sensations, because Wayne was ordering her to fix a salad, while he started charcoal for steaks.

"Steaks cooked on a grill? I thought I'd read somewhere that you were a gourmet cook."

"Actually I am," he called in from the patio, where he was struggling to light the charcoal. "But only when I have plenty of time to prepare the food and only when I have guests who will sit and savor every morsel. If you and I spend any time savoring anything tonight, it won't be the food."

Daring to meet the dangerous look he gave her, as he returned to the kitchen, she suggested sweetly, "Then why bother to eat at all?"

"Because, Miss Allen," he said very softly, "that is the civilized way to do things."

He walked to within a few inches of her, so close that she could feel the heat that radiated from his body. Leaning down, he whispered in her ear, "And, contrary to what you may believe, I am very, very civilized." Between words he nibbled on her ear provocatively, until Stacy thought her heart would explode in her chest. She was sure he must hear the blood pounding in her veins, as his lips met hers in a tender kiss.

"How do you like your sample of dessert?" he asked, kissing her lightly once more.

Indeed, the kiss seemed to have the sweetness of a honeyed dessert. But when Stacy would have tasted more, he pulled away.

"No more, Miss Allen. Haven't you heard? It'll ruin your appetite."

"I have a very healthy appetite, Congressman. A couple of little kisses won't spoil that."

"Well, I'm not taking any chances. You just keep chopping those vegetables."

"Haven't you heard that it's dangerous to deny a woman with a knife in her hand?" she asked lightly, brandishing the long, sharp blade.

"When you put it that way, how can I refuse?" he agreed, kissing her upturned nose, then darting back out to the patio before she could protest again.

While he was gone, Stacy found herself wondering at the camaraderie between them, after all that had happened. She hadn't expected to feel so completely at ease in this domestic setting. Nor had she thought she would be able to put aside all that she knew about Madeline Chase. In a way, it irked her that Wayne had an uncanny knack for breaking through her guard. He had only to look at her in that special way and she knew instantly she was his. There was a bond between them that no amount of tension and anger seemed able to destroy. If anything, it only served to enflame their passion.

Her thoughts were interrupted by Wayne's return.

"Ten more minutes," he informed her, as he started to carry silverware into the dining room.

"Let's eat in here," Stacy had suggested. "It's cozier."

"The housekeeper would be appalled," he said with

a shake of his head. "But if it's what you want, it's okay with me."

The light banter between them kept the atmosphere charged with an undercurrent of electricity throughout the meal. The salad was crisp, the baked potatoes oozed butter and sour cream, the steaks were rare and tender, but for Stacy it might as well have been gruel. She tasted nothing. Only the Cabernet Sauvignon had any effect on her and that went straight to her head in the kitchen's warmth. She was treading on dangerous ground now, but she no longer had the will to resist. Every fiber of her being longed for Wayne's touch.

As though in response to the thoughts tumbling around in her head, Wayne took her hand and held it while they ate, Stacy barely picking at her food.

"You're not eating," he observed, when he'd finished his own meal and noticed that hers was hardly touched.

"I'm not really hungry, I guess," she said, her voice an apologetic whisper.

"Then let's take the rest of the wine out to the patio," he suggested, pulling her to her feet.

Suddenly, irrationally reluctant, she asked, "What about the dishes?"

"What about them?" he asked with a grin.

"Shouldn't we wash them?"

"Stacy Allen, are you stalling?"

"Why would I be stalling?" she asked defensively. "I just thought we ought to stack the dishes in the sink at least."

"That's what I pay the housekeeper for," he insisted. "Now, come on. Let's go outside. It's a lovely night."

He was right, Stacy thought. It was a gorgeous evening. The moon was full, a scattering of stars twinkled in the distant darkness like tiny Christmas tree lights, and the air was filled with the scent of a potpourri of spring flowers.

They sat side by side on the redwood sofa, with its plump cushions covered in a brightly colored all-weather fabric. Wayne's arm was draped casually over her shoulder, holding her close to his side. Stacy found herself relaxing, giving in to the sensations stirred by his touch and the romantic setting.

Her body responding to him and her thoughts drifting, she was not prepared for the sharp change in Wayne's tone, when he said quietly, "Stacy we have to talk about some things."

When she would have drawn away, he held her tightly and insisted, "No. Come on. If we don't talk about these things, we'll never resolve them."

Stacy thought of the taxi driver who'd driven her home from Madeline Chase's party the previous night. That's what he'd said too. She allowed her body to relax again.

"Okay," she agreed with a small sigh.

"Let's start with Jay Lawrence. Where does he fit into your life?"

"I've already explained that," Stacy said, trying to keep the exasperation from her voice. "I worked for him in California. We're friendly, not really friends. That's all there is to it."

"Then why were you with him last night?" Wayne's tone was merely curious, but Stacy sensed a hidden threat in it. It was as though the wrong answer could spoil everything.

"Jay and I got used to doing things together in Los Angeles," she began slowly. "I suppose it was because we had no personal relationship. I was the perfect date. No demands. No need for devoted attention, It left him free to circulate without worrying about offending his date. If he got involved in something and didn't want to leave, I was perfectly capable and willing to get home on my own. He took me along last night for the same reason."

"What did you get out of all this?"

"Out there it was more or less part of my job. I could make contacts for him. And, from my own point of view, I got to meet some interesting, powerful people."

"But what about last night?" he asked, returning to his initial point. "You no longer work for Jay. Why did you agree to go with him to Madeline Chase's party?"

Stacy hesitated, knowing she could never tell him the whole truth, that she'd wanted to see for herself the woman she'd heard Wayne was involved with. She said only, "I'm not really sure. Curiosity, I suppose. It's the first of these big political affairs I've had a chance to attend."

Wayne was making it difficult for her to think about what she was saying. His hand was stroking her shoulder and arm, rising occasionally to trail seductively along the bare skin of her neck.

"I don't suppose you went with him last night, just to make me jealous?" he suggested.

Stacy couldn't imagine anything crazier. Why would her being there with Jay make him jealous? She had always made it perfectly clear what her relationship with Jay was. Even more important, it should be obvious to Wayne by now that she was in love with him. Why else would she even be here tonight?

There was a suggestion of disbelief in her voice, as she said, "Would my being there with Jay make you jealous? Honestly?"

"Yes, you little idiot."

"But, why?"

"Because, as I've mentioned repeatedly, I'm falling in love with you. I don't think I could bear the thought of losing you now."

His voice ended on something that sounded to Stacy's startled ears very much like a sob. Now her astonishment was complete.

"You really mean that, don't you?" she whispered urgently, hardly daring to hope that he would confirm it.

"I mean it," he said, gathering her into his arms in an embrace so tight, she could hardly breathe.

Then he was kissing her with a ferocious passion. The gentle, tender kisses they had shared in the past were replaced now by a hungry urgency, a demand for possession that almost frightened her with its intensity.

She found herself responding with total abandon. Her breasts strained against the thin material of her dress. Their sensitive peaks were fully aroused, awaiting the trembling delight of his touch.

She moved against him and, as they had in the car on that Sunday that now seemed so long ago, they were suddenly lying side by side, arms and legs entwined. Stacy's hands began a tentative exploration of their own, working the buttons of his shirt loose and reaching inside to feel with wonder the rough, hairy expanse of his chest, damp now with perspiration from the fiery heat of their passion.

He shifted slightly, but instead of being on top of her, he slipped off the sofa. A harsh laugh escaped from his lips.

"I see I've made another mistake in location," he said ruefully, looking up into her grinning face from the floor of the patio.

"Looks that way," she agreed, reaching out a hand to run her fingers through the tangled curls of his hair.

"You wouldn't want to come down here with me?" he asked hopefully.

She appeared to give the idea consideration. "Looks pretty uncomfortable to me," she concluded.

"Want to continue this discussion inside, then?"

"Is that what we're having?" she asked innocently. "A discussion? My momma never told me that discussions could be so stimulating."

"She didn't? That was terribly derelict of her. Never mind, though. Let me take you inside and demonstrate just how stimulating a discussion can become," he said, scooping her into his arms and walking with her into the house. As he carried her through the kitchen and dining room toward the stairs, she pounded on his shoulders.

"Put me down, you scoundrel," she insisted, unable to stop herself from laughing.

"Not a chance. I'm not putting you down, until I've found just the right spot this time."

As he spoke, a key rattled in the lock and Wayne froze, one foot on the stairway. Then the door was open and Madeline Chase was walking through it, a twisted mockery of a smile on her face, as she looked from Stacy to Wayne.

"Good evening, darling," Madeline said with syrupy sweetness. "I hope I wasn't intruding."

"What the hell are you doing here?" Wayne rasped angrily. "Where did you get a key?"

Stacy was fighting frantically to get out of Wayne's arms, but they were like iron bands around her. Overcome with fury and shocked at how willingly she had nearly given herself to him tonight, she wanted desperately to be away from him, away from this house, and away from this cheating woman.

"Don't play games, Wayne," she snapped bitterly. "You know damn good and well where she got the key."

Still struggling, she managed at last to land a blow that caused him to loosen his grip on her for an instant, long enough for her to slip from his arms. As though driven by demons, she raced to find her purse, straightening her rumpled clothes as she ran.

Wayne was running after her, but Madeline stepped in his path. "Darling, I do apologize for interrupting your . . . plans, but I had no idea . . ."

"You just be quiet and wait here," he demanded harshly. "I'll deal with you in a minute."

He almost caught up with Stacy on the patio, but she managed to unlock the rusty latch on the gate just as he came through the door. She sped through the gate into the alley, Wayne right on her heels.

"Stacy, you've got to listen to me," he said frantically, as she climbed into her car.

"Listen to you?" Her voice was incredulous. "I think I've already listened to your lies far too often. Go on back to your lover. You and I have nothing left to say to each other."

Wayne looked as though she had slapped him. "My lover?" he repeated in amazement. "Stacy, are you out of your mind?"

"Apparently," she said, turning on the car's engine.

"Stacy, please. You've got this all wrong."

"I doubt it."

Wayne's shoulders drooped dejectedly and his voice was filled with pain, as he said helplessly, "I see there's no point in trying to convince you of anything now, but there is an explanation and one of these days you'll have to listen to it."

"I'll never listen to another word you say, Congressman," she said coldly. "And, now, if you don't mind, I'd like to get the hell out of here."

She roared away from the parking space, nearly running a red light in her frantic desire to be as far from Wayne as possible. She wanted to be separated from him, as though that would rid her of this unbearable ache inside her. But as she calmed down and as the distance between them increased, she realized that it changed nothing. The pain remained and only time could ease it.

Eight

For the next few days Stacy was lost in a maze of tedious details, finalizing plans for her trip. Determined to bury that disastrous evening at Wayne's as deeply in her subconscious as possible, she doggedly took care of all the arrangements herself, declining all of Della's offers to help. The only thing she did permit Pete's secretary to do was answer her phone. It was the only way she could think of to avoid the repeated calls from Wayne. His messages were crumpled and tossed into the trash.

At home it was more difficult. She had more time to think and the constant, jarring ring of the phone ruined any chance she might have had of achieving tranquility. At times she felt like screaming, as the phone rang on and on, but she refused to answer it and give Wayne a chance to break down the protective barrier she was determined to erect between them. By Friday her nerves felt very close to the breaking point.

She arrived at National Airport only minutes before her flight time, hurried through the security check and ran down the concourse to the gate. Most of the passengers were already on board by the time she checked in and made her way to the plane's coach section.

Glancing around, she noticed that the plane wasn't crowded and she slipped into her window seat with a grateful sigh of relief. It looked as though she would have the entire row of seats to herself, she thought thankfully, as she pulled a paperback novel from her flight bag before stuffing the bag under the seat in front of her. Maybe the book would be a distraction from her uncomfortable thoughts during the long flight.

She settled back in her seat and watched the ground crew outside finish its work. The crew had just finished loading the luggage, when she heard someone slip into the aisle seat in her row. Inwardly, she groaned at the thought of the intrusion, praying that the person wouldn't chatter from Washington to Los Angeles. All she wanted for the next five hours was to be left alone.

Peeking surreptitiously to her right, she let out a shocked gasp.

"You!"

"Hi, Stacy," Wayne replied calmly, as though nothing had happened at their last encounter. He sorted through the papers in his briefcase as nonchalantly as if she were a total stranger. Or as though he had expected to find her there.

Whatever the explanation, Stacy had no intention of sticking around to discover it. Frantically she began gathering her things, but when she stood and tried to step past him to the aisle, he refused to budge. And, unless he moved his long legs, there was no way she could exit without climbing onto the middle seat and stepping unceremoniously over him.

"Let me out of here," she hissed softly.

"Sorry," he said, not even looking up.

"Wayne Dodge, let me out or I'll call the stewardess," she threatened, an edge of hysteria creeping into her voice. She was beginning to feel that same panicky desperation to escape she had felt earlier in the week, when Madeline Chase had walked in on them at Wayne's.

There was a defiant gleam in Wayne's eyes at her challenge.

"Go ahead," he said, as though it couldn't possibly matter to him one way or the other. "Call her."

Stacy reached for the call button, but after several seconds of standing there, her outstretched hand trembling, she couldn't bring herself to ring it. Defeated, she sank weakly into her seat blinking back tears of frustration, hurt, and anger.

"Why?" she asked, her voice a desperate cry. "Why are you here? Why are you doing this?"

"The same reason you are, I suppose," he said with feigned innocence. "I'm on my way to Los Angeles."

"But why today? This flight? Why this seat?"

His eyes met hers unblinkingly. "You want the answers in any particular order?"

"It doesn't matter," she said flatly.

"I always fly on Friday afternoon on this flight. I am in this seat because I asked for it."

She stared at him blankly for a moment, then recalled his reaction on discovering that she was seated next to him. He hadn't been surprised. It was just as she'd thought earlier: He'd expected her to be there.

"You knew that I would be here?"

He nodded.

"But how?"

"Della told me. We've gotten to be very friendly over the last few days. She recognizes a man in love when she hears one. She couldn't resist telling me you'd be taking this flight to Los Angeles this afternoon. After that it was easy. When you fly frequently, the airline will accommodate almost any reasonable request."

"And you asked for the seat next to mine."

"Exactly," he said, nodding as though she were a very bright student who'd just caught on to a complicated theory.

"But what's the point?" she asked. "You know I don't want to see you. I certainly don't want to spend the next five hours sitting next to you or talking to you."

"That's exactly the point. You have repeatedly refused to answer my calls. I suspect you've been sitting home every evening listening to the damn phone ring off the hook, just because you won't face up to this ridiculous problem you've created between us."

Stacy was incredulous. "I've created!" she nearly shouted. "I didn't create the problem, Congressman. You did. Madeline Chase is your monster, not mine. Oh, what's the use," she said flatly, turning her back on him. "Just leave me alone."

"I'll leave you alone . . . for now," he agreed placidly. "But it's a long flight, Stacy. Sooner or later, we're going to work this out. By the time we get to Los Angeles, you're going to grow up and tell me what the hell this is all about!"

Then, to her utter amazement, he pulled down his tray table and went to work, ignoring her just as she'd demanded. But instead of being happy about being left alone, she found his silence even more irritating than their crazy conversation.

Why couldn't he understand why she was so angry? She had every right to be furious, she reasoned. Was he so amoral that he found nothing wrong with having a fling with a married woman, while professing to love another woman?

She stole a quick glance at his clean-shaven profile, with its slightly rugged look. He was frowning now in concentration and there were tiny furrows in his forehead that Stacy's hand itched to smooth away. The tangy scent of his after-shave drifted over to her, a subtle reminder of being held in his arms, close to the warm, musky smell of his masculinity.

Her eyes drifted to his hands, the long tapered fingers flecked with dark hairs. They were gentle, sensitive hands. She recalled the sensations they had stirred in her and a liquid warmth spread through her body. She shifted restlessly in her seat.

Damn, she thought. Why didn't he look up? Talk to her again? Her mind reeled with these contradictory desires. First she wanted no part of him. Then, only to be held in his arms once again. What was wrong with her?

He seemed to sense her mood at last and he lifted his gaze from his papers and met her eyes. A slow, sensuous smile spread across his face, a smile that made her heart lurch. But then he went back to work, his head bowed over the stack of papers scattered on the tray in front of him and tumbling haphazardly into the seat between them. That seat seemed to separate them as convincingly as any ocean. Stacy felt as though they'd never close the distance between them.

The thought set her teeth on edge. Every fiber of her being was directly in tune with the man sitting only a foot or two away and yet he might as well have been on the other side of the world. Each of his movements increased her restlessness until she prayed for something, anything to end this unbearable silence.

She pulled out a paperback novel and tried to

concentrate on the complicated plot. But the thriller was no match for real life. Her own plight seemed far more precarious than the heroine's. She was in danger of giving in to her emotions again, in danger of allowing Wayne to convince her their relationship had a chance, when she knew it had none at all.

The rattle of the drink cart distracted her from the page she'd been staring at blindly for several minutes. Wayne was smiling at the stewardess.

"Hi, Congressman!" she said enthusiastically. "Going home for the weekend again?"

"Yeah. Have to let the folks out there know what I've been up to. They don't trust anyone who stays in Washington too long. How've you been Karen?"

"Just fine, but I'll be glad to get home again. I've been in the air more than I've been on the ground the last few weeks. A couple of the girls were out sick and I had to fill in."

The stewardess was efficiently filling drink orders for the people across the aisle as she talked to Wayne. Finishing the last of them, she asked him, "You want your usual?"

"That'll be fine." He turned to Stacy. "What about you?"

For a moment she was seized by such an irrational surge of jealousy that she was afraid to speak. At last, ignoring Wayne, she said curtly, "I'd like a Scotch on the rocks, please. In fact, make it two of them."

She pulled the dollar bills from her purse, but Wayne had already paid the stewardess and the cart had moved along to the next row of seats.

"I don't want you to buy my drinks," she said, knowing she was being absurd.

He shrugged. "Fine," he agreed, taking the crumpled bills from her and stuffing them into his pocket. "You realize, of course, that you're being ridiculous again?"

Hearing the charge from him only infuriated her more.

"Why am I the one who's being ridiculous?" she demanded, drinking down half of one of the Scotches in a single gulp.

"Suppose you tell me," he countered. "I sure as hell can't figure it out."

"This is getting us nowhere," Stacy muttered in disgust.

"I agree."

"Wayne," she said, her voice pleading.

Their eyes locked and a blazing light seemed to fill them. Relenting at last, he dropped his combative posture and reached over and took her hand, holding it tightly.

"Think we can talk about it now?" he asked gently. Then, looking at the second drink in her hand, he added, "Before you get plastered."

"I am not about to get plastered," she insisted defensively.

"Are you used to drinking this much liquor in a five minute period then? I'm surprised."

"No," she admitted reluctantly. "I don't usually drink this stuff at all. But being around you gives me an unreasonable urge to . . . I don't know . . . escape, maybe."

"You won't find your escape in that glass, Stacy," he said, taking it from her hand. "In fact, if you'll only be honest with yourself, you don't really want to escape from me at all. Do you?" When she didn't answer, he insisted, "Do you, Stacy?"

"Maybe not," she conceded softly, then added with a note of desperation, "but I have to."

"Why?"

"Because it can't work, Wayne. It can't and you know it."

"I don't know anything of the sort. In fact, since

we are several thousand feet in the air, where no one can hear us, I propose to tell you once more that I am in love with you."

"No," she cried out. "Please. Don't say that."

"I'm going to say it, Stacy, and you're going to listen. I love you. I've always loved you, from that very first minute I saw you in that restaurant. Sooner or later you'll admit you feel the same way. Right now you're just being stubborn."

Withdrawing her hand from his grip, she asked quietly, "What about Madeline Chase?"

"What about her? You keep bringing her up, as though she's supposed to mean something to me. She's a friend, a desperate, lonely friend. Nothing more."

Stacy studied him closely, looking for some sign that would betray him, give away the lie. There was none and she dared to hope.

"Do you mean that?" she asked breathlessly.

"Of course, I mean it. What else could she be?"

"She's in love with you. The rumor is that the two of you are having a heavy affair right under her husband's nose."

There was a long hesitation before Wayne spoke again, an instant in which Stacy felt her heart clutched in the grasp of fear.

"Maybe she is in love with me," Wayne admitted slowly. "But, Stacy, I am not in love with her and there is no affair."

He forced her to look at him. "Do you understand me? There is no affair."

"But you're together . . . a lot. I've seen you. She has the key to your house . . . the rumors." She came to a stuttering halt.

"The rumors are just that . . . rumors. As for the key, she got it from the housekeeper without telling me. Mrs. Mason knows Madeline's a close friend and she let her have it. She doesn't have it anymore. As for the time we spend together, it's just what I told you before—she is a desperately lonely woman. Her husband is terribly ill and neither of them will admit to the other that they know it. She turns to me when she needs to talk. That's all there is to it."

"But she told me—"

"Told you what?" he demanded.

"She told me to stay away from you, that you were hers."

Shock registered on his face. "She told you that?" he asked incredulously. "When?"

"The night of her party."

"So that was it," he said in sudden understanding. "It all makes sense now. Stacy, I swear to you again that there is nothing between Madeline Chase and me. I'll talk to her. I'll even get her to tell you the truth, if it's what you want. Maybe she does have some crazy idea about being in love with me, but she has no claim on me, no right to talk to you that way. I'll make her understand that. I promise you."

All the fear and anger drained out of Stacy at his words, leaving her weak with relief. Wayne wasn't involved with Madeline Chase. The thought elated her. And, if that was true, then maybe he was telling the truth about loving her as well.

When she looked at him, the emotion she saw burning in his eyes certainly could be love. His eyes seemed to devour her. That look was filled with as much passion, as much intensity as any touch. It lasted for a long, breathless moment.

And, then, it was as though a dam had burst. With all of their self-imposed constraints removed, they talked for the first time in days. It was a crazy, happy conversation that wandered directionless from one subject to another, as though to make up for all that lost time.

For the time being there was no thought of what this newly-admitted love would do to her documentary. She wanted only to revel in the topsy-turvy sensations she was feeling, to share this exquisite joy with the man she loved. Wayne seemed to be feeling this same exuberance, this same excitement.

"Stacy, there's so much I want to show you this weekend. I want you to meet my family, some of my friends. Or would you rather just be together? You don't have plans, do you?" he asked anxiously.

"Well," she said slowly, "I did have a couple of dates."

"Cancel them," he ordered brusquely.

She grinned. "I suppose I might be able to change them . . . for the right incentive."

He leaned across and kissed her soundly.

"Is that incentive enough?"

"Not bad," she teased. "That should get me out of tonight's date, but I'm not so sure about Saturday and Sunday."

"Listen, young lady, cancel your plans or I'll be forced to camp out on your doorstep and beat the men up as they arrive. That certainly wouldn't do your reputation much good."

"Yours either," she admonished him.

"The satisfaction might be worth it."

"Never mind. Get your kicks some other way, I'll change my plans, but only because I'd rather be with you. Not because you ordered me to do it. Understand?"

"Absolutely," he said, a mocking grin on his face.

Wayne's mounting enthusiasm about their weekend plans delighted Stacy. It was a whole new side to him, this childlike excitement about showing off his other life, sharing it with her.

"You'll love my house, Stacy. It's not at all like the one in Georgetown. It's very modern, very simple. It's right on the beach. We can have breakfast on the patio in the morning and then go for a long walk."

"Hey, slow down, Congressman. Who said anything about my staying at your house?"

"Where else would you stay?"

"I have a perfectly good hotel reservation."

"Just call and say you won't be needing it."

"I can't do that," she said stubbornly.

"Why on earth not?" he exploded. "You're a big girl, Stacy, and it's no longer the Victorian age. It's perfectly respectable for you to stay at the beach with me."

"I'm not sure how respectable it is, but that's not the issue," she insisted. "The station made the hotel reservation and the news department's paying for it. If Pete doesn't get a bill, he'll wonder where I stayed instead. I don't think he'd like the answer if it turned out to be your place."

Wayne's expression, which had grown stormy, softened. "Is that all? I thought you were just trying to back out on me again."

"I'm not trying to back out of anything. I'm just trying to be sensible, which, I might add, is not so easy with you around."

"Just to prove that I can be as sensible as the next man, I have your solution. All you need to do is register at the hotel before we go out to Malibu. You can call in for messages and the station will have no idea you were anywhere other than safely tucked in your room."

Stacy considered the idea carefully, looking for flaws. "Okay," she agreed at last. "Let me check in, leave some of my things in the room, and attend to a few scheduling details. Then I'll come with you."

Wayne reached over and squeezed her hand.

"You won't regret it. We'll have a wonderful week-end. I promise."

Nine

The weekend had turned out to be nearly idyllic, a dreamlike escape from reality that Stacy knew would be hard to recapture, even if they spent a lifetime together. From the time they arrived at the beach house late Friday night until he had taken her back to her hotel on Sunday, there had been only one fleeting misunderstanding to disrupt their happiness. And even that had been smoothed away easily enough, once they had brought it into the open and talked it through.

The house itself was nothing like she had expected, even after Wayne's description on the plane. It was small, its proportions almost dollhouse-sized. Wayne's long-legged strides through its rooms seemed to reduce them to no more than closets and yet it wasn't claustrophobic at all.

The entire western wall of the living room was glass, overlooking a deck that was surrounded by vibrant splashes of color, as flowers tumbled over the side walls.

The blue-green of the Pacific was just beyond,

separated from the house by a wide stretch of beach, rolling with dunes. The roar of the tumbling waves created a melodic background tune for them.

Inside the house, the bright, airy rooms seemed more spacious than they were, thanks to the clean spare lines of the Scandinavian furniture, the earth-tone fabrics, and the thriving plants that provided the only decorations. There was a tiny kitchen, plus two bedrooms, each with its own bath. The chauffeur had put their luggage in separate rooms, then discreetly left them on their own. In an odd way, Stacy had been reluctant to see him leave.

Once he was gone, her nervousness returned. She knew it was a combination of fear at the thought of being alone with Wayne and of anxiety over their deception. She still wasn't convinced their ploy about the hotel would work. She'd felt guilty ever since she'd walked out the front door, her clothes stuffed in what she hoped the hotel doorman and anyone else who'd seen them would assume was simply an oversized purse.

Still, she found herself pacing from room to room, unable to sit down and relax as Wayne made call after call from the phone in the living room. He seemed oblivious to her growing panic. Catching her eye between calls, he suggested she look in the refrigerator for something they could have for a late dinner. Without noticing the icy glare she gave him, he promptly dialed another call.

Irritated at what she perceived to be a total lack of sensitivity, Stacy rebelliously retreated to what was apparently the guest room and unpacked the few things she'd brought from the hotel. Unfortunately for her peace of mind, the task took only a few minutes and did nothing to alleviate her sense of being abandoned.

Rather than going into the kitchen as Wayne had

ordered her to do, she decided, instead, to prolong her rebellion by taking a shower. Maybe it would also serve to relax her. In the tiny stall, the hot water flowed over her, easing the knotted muscles in her shoulders and neck. The sudsy lather she had worked up from head to toe washed away, leaving her skin feeling silky and alive. Her breasts tingled under the sharp, stinging spray of the water.

When she turned off the water at last, the bathroom was steamy. Reaching out, she grabbed the fluffy brown towel and then stepped from the stall. Her hair was sparkling with drops of water and her skin was a rosy pink. Suddenly, she felt wonderful again. It was going to be a glorious weekend after all. She would see to it. She glanced in the mirror and froze. Wayne was staring at her, a wicked grin on his face.

"What are you doing in here?" she gasped, clutching the towel more tightly around her.

"Looking for you," he said casually, leaning against the door frame.

"Well, now you've found me, so get out and let me get dressed."

"Sure you don't want me to stay and rub your back dry?" he suggested with a roguish gleam in his eye.

"I've done very well all these years on my own, thank you. I'll do it myself."

"Perhaps you don't know what you've been missing then," he said softly, picking up another towel and vigorously rubbing her shoulders. After a few strokes there was a subtle shift in his movements and what had begun as simply drying her back altered into a sensuous massage.

"Wayne, please," Stacy begged, her voice ragged and panicky. "Let me get dressed."

Stilled by her request, his hands remained on her

shoulders. Then, after what seemed an eternity, he removed them.

"Okay . . . for now," he said quietly.

Stacy stood with her back toward him, afraid to move. She didn't anticipate what he was about to do and when the stinging slap of the towel hit her bottom, she whirled toward him.

"Why you . . . you rat," she screamed, chasing him into the bedroom.

"What did I do?" he asked with feigned innocence from the corner into which she'd backed him. Without giving it a second thought, she took her own towel and delivered a stinging slap of her own.

"That," she said, delighted at his startled expression.

Then, suddenly, her delight changed to alarm, as she realized what she had done. She was standing in front of him completely naked. Frantically, she tried to retrieve the towel, but he wouldn't release it.

Like a startled doe, she stood indecisively before him, unsure what to do next. Then she turned and fled into the bathroom, slamming and locking the door behind her.

When he pounded on the door, she shouted, "Go away!"

"Stacy, it's okay," he said soothingly, as though talking to a frightened child. "Really. Come back out, please."

"Not until you leave," she whispered, her cheek pressed against the cool wood of the door.

She was still flushed with embarrassment and something else, some sensation aroused by the look she had seen in his eyes, as they roved thirstily over her bare skin. A flame of unmistakable desire had been lit, threatening to burst into a raging fire if she didn't find some way to quench it. What terrified her was the thought that she didn't really want to quench it at all. She wanted to experience the full heat of his passion. And, yet, she had run away.

Trembling, she stood there waiting for him to leave the bedroom. At last she heard his retreating footsteps and she crept out and put on her clothes, a pair of jeans and a bulky sweater designed to camouflage rather than enhance her curves. Stacy glossed lightly over her lips with a pale shade of lipstick and put a dab of mascara on her lashes before daring to venture into the living room. Her cheeks needed no extra color. Not tonight, certainly.

Almost timidly she went into the living room to find Wayne busy lighting a fire, as though he'd forgotten all about the incident in the bedroom.

"Did you ever look in the refrigerator?" he asked casually over his shoulder.

"Not yet. I'll do it now," she said quickly, grateful to have something specific to do to relieve the awkwardness she was feeling.

She was surprised to find the shelves of the refrigerator loaded with food. There were eggs, various cheeses, vegetables, fruit, and an assortment of things to drink, including fresh-squeezed orange juice. The freezer was stocked just as temptingly. There were clearly labeled packages of meat, as well as several casseroles in dishes large enough to hold a meal for two.

"See anything you'd like?" Wayne asked, staying a circumspect distance from her, as though aware of the emotional war that was being waged within her.

"If you're not starved, how about something simple like an omelette. It's awfully late for a big meal."

"Fine. I'll see if there's some fresh bread in there. Paul's wife usually bakes some and leaves it in the freezer. Yep," he said, pulling out a long, foil-wrapped loaf. "Here it is."

"Is the refrigerator always this well stocked, so

you can walk in anytime and put a perfect meal on the table?"

"Always. Mary sees to it. She takes anything perishable home with her after I leave, but the other food stays. She's quite a cook. Wait'll you taste some of her casseroles. The lasagna is better than any I've had in a restaurant."

"My mouth's watering. Maybe we should have that instead?" she suggested hopefully.

"You're the one who said it was too late for a hearty meal. I can eat lasagna anytime."

Stacy looked longingly at the freezer, then shook her head.

"No. I was right the first time. It's too late for that. We'll have the omelette."

While she cracked the eggs and whipped them with the wire whisk, Wayne opened a bottle of white wine. After he'd poured them each a glass, he flipped on the stereo, choosing a quiet classical album that Stacy found incredibly soothing. Once again, he had found a way to make her relax and feel at ease with him.

Hungrily, they ate the omelette and the fresh bread, warmed in the oven. They lingered over the wine, opening up to each other about their hopes and dreams.

"I can't remember a time, when I didn't want to be a reporter," Stacy said. "It wasn't so much the glamour of it, ironically, though goodness knows you get to meet some fascinating people. I guess I just wanted to satisfy my curiosity about the way the world runs. I figured if I had questions, other people must have them too. I wanted to find the answers."

"Has it been all you thought it would be?"

"Most of the time. I was very idealistic, though. I wasn't prepared for the compromises we make sometimes. I thought we'd always be noble, no matter who got hurt in the process. Tell the truth at any cost. I'm beginning to see that's not always the best way. There are things the public doesn't need to know. What worries me is who will decide which things those are. I trust people like Pete to do the right thing. I'm not sure about some others."

"I'm glad you're not always so sure of everything anymore," he teased. "That would be very hard to take."

"You're right," she agreed, laughing. "I was pretty impossible."

"How about a walk on the beach?" he suggested then, pulling her to her feet.

They went on a long, leisurely stroll, giggling as they stumbled over sand dunes. Holding hands, they hardly spoke at all, enveloped in the night's companionable, silent embrace.

Back at the house, he bent to kiss her, a lingering kiss that oddly made no demands.

"It's late, Stacy," he said, holding her loosely in his arms. "Go on to bed."

She looked up at him questioningly.

"Go on," he insisted harshly. "Before I change my mind."

"But . . ." she began hesitantly, not knowing the words to say what she wanted to. "I thought . . ."

"So did I," he said curtly. "But I've changed my mind. Go in the house."

There was an edge to his voice that kept her from arguing any further. Tears welling up in her eyes, she refused to let him see how hurt and confused she was. She walked away stiffly and went to the guest room.

Instead of sleeping, she tossed and turned most of the night, her mind whirling in its search for answers to explain his unfathomable behavior. She was still awake at 4:00 A.M., when she heard him go into his room, muttering under his breath as he bumped into something. Obviously, he was in no better shape than she was.

"Damn," she said aloud. It hadn't needed to be this way, she thought in frustration. She had made a commitment to him simply by coming here. Why hadn't he wanted her to keep it?

No logical explanations came to her and finally, shortly before dawn, she fell into a restless sleep. Bright sunlight streaming into the room woke her only a few hours later. Still feeling groggy, she groaned and rolled over, but it was no use. She was awake to stay.

Stretching, she got out of bed and into the same jeans and sweater she'd worn the night before. Quickly she made the bed, splashed some cool water on her face and ran a comb through her tangled hair. A touch of lipstick and she felt almost human.

Barefoot, she padded into the living room and gazed out toward the ocean in wonder. It was dancing with a sparkling iridescence in the early morning sun. The wide beach was practically deserted except for an occasional jogger and an older couple, who appeared to be looking for shells. She slid open the door and sniffed the brisk, salty air.

How could anyone not find contentment here, she thought to herself as she went into the kitchen to plug in the coffee pot and pour herself a large glass of orange juice. She drank that, while the coffee perked, filling the house with its rich fragrance. When the coffee was ready, she took a cup with her to the patio.

Dragging a chair to a corner that was already touched by the sun, she leaned back and turned her face toward its warmth. Although the early morning air was still chilly, the sun felt like a cozy blanket.

Wrapped in its comforting embrace, she fell at last into a deep sleep.

Sometime later she awoke with a start, when she felt something tickling her nose. Sleepily, she waved her hand to brush it away, but as soon as her hand moved away, the tickling sensation returned. She opened one eye to take a peek at her tormentor and discovered Wayne standing over her.

"Good morning, sleeping beauty," he said, leaning down to kiss her more solidly on the mouth. "We have more comfortable beds in the house, you know."

"But this one has a better blanket," she said, gesturing lazily toward the sun.

"Want some juice?" he asked, holding out his own glass.

"I've had some."

"What about more coffee?"

"No, thanks," she said, stretching like a graceful cat, as her eyes drifted shut once more.

"Hey!" he said, shaking her. "You're not going back to sleep, are you? We have things to do today. We can't waste the whole day just lazing around."

"What things?" she asked suspiciously.

"I thought we'd go for a swim, then a long walk. After lunch we can go sailing with some friends of mine. They invited us last night."

"Where did you come up with all this energy? I thought you'd be exhausted today."

"I never get much sleep. I don't seem to need it."

"Well, I do," she said, closing her eyes again.

"I see," he said slowly, as though considering their options. "How about going for the swim and the walk and skipping the sailing?"

She peeked at him from under the arm she was holding across her eyes to block the sun. "I guess that's fair. Are you sure you don't mind about the sailing?"

He grinned. "Actually, no. I'd rather keep you here all to myself."

She returned his gaze evenly and that current of electricity seemed to leap between them. "Me too," she admitted softly.

He came to sit on the edge of her lounge chair, his body pressed against her side. One hand gently brushed the curls back from her face, then traced its planes, as though he were a blind man trying to discover by touch how she looked. As his fingers trailed tantalizingly across her lips, she captured his hand and held it, whispering against it, "Wayne."

"What?"

"Can I ask you a question?"

"Anything."

For a fraction of a second she hesitated, then asked boldly, "What happened last night? Why did you change your mind?"

A look of pain flashed in his eyes as he stared beyond her toward the ocean. When he looked at her again, the pain was gone and in its place was a tender smile.

"That was the hardest thing I've ever had to do in my life," he said, his hand resuming its gentle stroking of her lips, her face, her neck. "It took every ounce of willpower in me to send you into the house alone."

"Then why did you do it?"

"Because you're not ready yet. There have been a lot of complications in our relationship. There still are. I want all of those resolved, all of the doubts removed before anything happens between us. I want you to trust me completely, to want me as much as I want you."

"But I do," she said with total conviction.

"No, you don't," he countered, putting a finger over her lips, when she would have interrupted him.

"You don't yet, Stacy. If you did, you wouldn't have been so terrified when I walked in on you in the bathroom last night."

"I was just surprised, that's all," she argued.

"No. You were panicky. I could see it in your eyes." His hand came to rest on the side of her face, while his thumb teased her lips. "Besides, we have plenty of time."

"You mean this weekend?"

"I mean a lifetime," he whispered, kissing her lightly.

Then he was standing, tugging her up from the lounge.

"Come on. That's enough of this soul-searching stuff for this morning. The day is going to be half over before we even go for a swim. Get your bathing suit on."

Wayne's reassurance that nothing would happen between them until she was ready for it removed the subtle pressure Stacy had been feeling. His words were like a tranquilizer, soothing her into a relaxed state that allowed her to totally abandon her guard with him. For the rest of the day they swam, walked hand in hand along the beach, sat side by side on the patio and talked. It was an extension of the previous night's directionless conversation, at times delving into deep personal beliefs and at others skimming superficially over inconsequential things. It was a day punctuated with laughter and as the sun sank slowly, turning the Pacific into a sea of gold and orange, Stacy felt happier than she ever had before.

As dusk began to settle around them, Wayne asked, "What about dinner? Want to go out?"

"Not unless you do."

"Afraid the real world will spoil our fantasy?" he teased.

"Maybe," she admitted, returning his smile.

"Trust me. It won't. Let's put it to a test."

"Okay," she agreed. "But nothing fancy."

"I know the perfect seafood restaurant just down the road a few miles. We may have to wait, but the food is terrific."

"Do I have to dress up?"

"You really are getting lazy, young lady, but, no, jeans will do. This place isn't noted for its ambiance."

An hour later they were ready to leave. Freshly showered, Wayne's hair was still damp and Stacy felt an irresistible urge to brush it back from his forehead. Standing on tiptoe, she smoothed the strands from his face, then kissed him lightly. The masculine scent of his after-shave filled her nostrils, acting almost like a heady aphrodisiac as it stirred her senses alive. She clung to him, hungrily tasting his lips.

When she broke free at last, Wayne's expression was shaken.

"What was that all about?"

She tried to seem nonchalant, though her heart seemed to be pounding at a frantic pace. "Just a sudden urge," she said as casually as she could manage.

"Any more urges like that one and all my good intentions will go right out the window," he warned, a wickedly possessive gleam in his eyes.

"I'll keep that in mind," she replied with a grin, before kissing him quickly again and then walking out the door.

"You're tempting fate, woman," Wayne said, as he followed her to the garage and climbed into a small, dark green Triumph.

When he'd backed out of the driveway onto the road, Stacy got in and they drove along the coast south through Santa Monica. When they reached the restaurant a short time later, they found it already jammed, just as Wayne had expected.

They found a table on the front porch, which served as a bar and waiting area, and ordered wine to drink while they waited.

"I'm surprised you're willing to hang around like this just to get dinner," Stacy said.

"I do get impatient when I have something pressing to do, but tonight there's no rush. As long as we're together, what difference does it make whether we're out here having a drink or in there?"

"A very romantic attitude, Congressman. I'm impressed."

"You should be. You're the one responsible. Before I met you I rarely spent more than a few hours with a woman without being bored to tears."

"Even in bed?" Stacy asked daringly.

"Even there," he insisted.

"But you must know lots of fascinating, successful women. How could you possibly have been bored with them?"

"Some of them were intellectually stimulating, but that wears thin after awhile, unless they're also desirable. It's a rare combination. You're one of the few women I've met who is both bright and sexually appealing. That's a pretty potent threat to an old bachelor like me."

Stacy knew what he meant. What they shared was more than a mere physical attraction. It was a powerful force, fueled by chemistry and a shared intellectual curiosity. It was far different from the feelings she had had for other men in her life and she was already learning to value it as something exceptional and special.

Inside the restaurant a few minutes later, they

ordered fresh snapper, which was broiled to moist, flaky perfection and served with cole slaw and potato salad. Stacy hadn't realized how hungry she was until the food was in front of her. She ate every morsel with barely a word. When she finished, she looked over to find Wayne regarding her with an amused smile.

"Hungry?" he asked.

She laughed. "I must have been starved."

"I'm not surprised. It's been a busy day and we haven't eaten much. Want dessert?"

"No. I think I've filled all the empty spaces," she said.

"Coffee?"

"Nope."

"Then let's get out of here," he suggested, beckoning for their waitress.

Stacy sensed in him an impatience and realized she shared that same desire to return to their earlier isolation and intimacy. This dinner hadn't spoiled things, just as Wayne had promised it wouldn't, but she had a longing to retreat once more from the real world. These fantasy days would end far too soon as it was.

"Let's go home," he said softly, taking her hand and leading her to the car.

Odd, Stacy thought to herself, as they drove north, retracing their earlier route, how she too had come to think of the beach house as home. Before she could give the matter too much thought, though, she was asleep, worn out by the fresh ocean air, the long walks and the swims. The next thing she knew, they were in the driveway and Wayne was picking her up in his arms.

"Where are we?" she murmured, sleepily.

"Home," he whispered, carrying her around to the front door.

She snuggled into his arms and nuzzled her face against his neck, her breath a soft, gentle touch against his skin.

"You're not playing fair, Stacy," he said hoarsely, but he did nothing to stop her disturbing behavior. He carried her directly to the guest room and placed her gently on the bed. For a moment it seemed she wasn't going to release the grip she had around his neck, but he eased her hands loose, brushed his lips across hers lightly and crept out, taking a deep, ragged breath as he closed the door quietly behind him.

As soon as he had gone, Stacy breathed a contented sigh and snuggled down, her arms wrapped around a pillow. Already she was dreaming, lovely, happy dreams filled with images of Wayne. In each of them she felt safe, protected, adored. When she awoke in the morning to the scent of bacon and coffee, those feelings stayed with her.

She hummed as she showered and dressed, anticipating the day that stretched ahead. Not even the gray, leaden skies and sheets of rain could dampen her mood, she thought as she went into the kitchen, where Wayne was scrambling eggs to go with the bacon she had smelled. Toast, juice, and a pot of homemade strawberry jam were already on the table.

"You've been busy this morning," Stacy said, sniffing appreciatively.

"And you've been very lazy," he admonished her, pausing on his way to the table to give her a quick peck on the cheek. "I had to do something dramatic to tempt you out of bed."

"That's a switch."

"What do you mean?"

She grinned up at him impudently. "You're usually trying to tempt me into bed."

"Cute, lady. Get to the table and behave yourself

or I may decide to replace the breakfast menu I've prepared with something a little sweeter," he warned with a devilish leer.

"Yes, sir. No problem. I'm ravenous," she agreed, sitting down as she'd been told to do.

After breakfast, they did the dishes together, bantering the whole time. The domestic atmosphere, charged with an undercurrent of electricity, began to stir a mix of emotions in Stacy. She dreaded its inevitable end and yet she feared what would happen if it went on beyond today. There were still far too many implications for her to feel entirely comfortable about this growing relationship.

She had the rest of the morning to think about her concerns. Wayne was absorbed in the paperwork he had brought along and she'd been left to her own devices. She tried to read the paperback she'd been unable to follow on the plane, but once more her concentration deserted her. Instead, her eyes strayed from its pages to watch as Wayne absentmindedly ran his fingers through his hair, as he read over the stack of reports prepared by his staff. His ability to absorb the material quickly was a marvel to her. He seemed to reach decisions almost instantly, jotting notations on the material and moving on to the next report. His pile of finished work grew rapidly, while the pages of Stacy's book barely turned at all.

At last he took out a legal-size yellow pad and began scribbling furiously, as though some anger deep inside was being spilled onto the page. Stacy wanted to peek over his shoulder, but she was afraid he wouldn't welcome the distraction.

Finally he sighed deeply and turned to her.

"Want to take a look at this and see what you think?"

"Sure," she said, going to his side. "What is it?"

"A speech I'm making next week on the mistreatment of illegal aliens."

"You write your own speeches?" Stacy asked, surprised at the discovery. Most politicians had a whole staff of speech writers to draw upon.

"I have a writer on my staff, but I prefer to do the really important speeches myself. He does some of the research, but I usually put it into my own words."

"Let me see," she said, looking over his shoulder.

It was an impassioned speech, decrying the employers who were capitalizing on the poor men and women who had slipped across the border from Mexico in desperation and were now being used by these callous employers as cheap labor. It was a cry from the heart and painted such a devastating picture that it made Stacy want to weep. There were tears in her eyes when she reached the conclusion, which called for tougher laws against those who exploited the desperate.

"Well, what do you think?"

"It's wonderful."

"Think it'll change anything?" he asked doubtfully.

"How could anyone listen to this and not want to do something? It has to bring about change," Stacy said with certainty.

"Optimist," he said with a trace of sarcasm and bitterness. "I hope you're right, though. These things need to happen."

Stacy couldn't resist putting her hand against his cheek in a gesture of comfort. He grinned up at her, then, and his tone was lighter as he suggested, "How about dinner with my parents tonight? You up to the inquisition?"

Stacy felt a nervous fluttering in her stomach, but

she said bravely, "Sure, if you think it's a good idea."

"Absolutely." Then, noticing her expression, "Hey, it'll be okay. They'll adore you."

"Okay, then. Will we be coming back here?"

"No. I'll have to drop you off at the hotel right after dinner, so I can catch the red eye back to Washington."

"Oh," she said, unable to keep the note of sadness and disappointment from her voice.

"Don't look so dejected," he said, squeezing her hand. "We'll be back here again."

Stacy seized the promise, but she couldn't help taking a longing look around the room, bright once more with the sunlight that was breaking through the clouds.

"It's been so perfect," she sighed.

He pulled her onto his lap and held her. "It has been, hasn't it?" he said gently, his hand lightly cupping her breast. He began a slow massage that made her moan softly.

"Wayne," she whispered brokenly, lowering her lips to his with a greediness that shocked her with its intensity.

"My God, Stacy," he groaned, his mouth hard against hers. Just when their passion would have flared into an all-consuming fire, he stood her on her feet.

"Enough," he said gruffly, his tone softening at her look of hurt. With a smile, he added, "Any more of this and we'll never leave here at all."

"Would that be so awful?" she asked wishfully.

"No, but it wouldn't be real. Reality is putting all of this together with our other obligations. It'll work just fine, Stacy. I promised you that before, and I meant it."

She clung to him tightly, her face pressed against the soft cotton of his shirt.

What will I do, if he can't keep that promise? she wondered, trying to stem the panicky feeling the thought evoked.

Ten

No matter how hard she tried, Stacy wasn't able to overcome a feeling that things were about to change drastically for her and Wayne and that there was absolutely nothing she could do to prevent it. It was a feeling that left her shaken and she looked back toward the house with a yearning expression, as they drove away.

"Sad thoughts again?" Wayne inquired tenderly.

Stacy nodded.

"Why? I've made you a promise, haven't I?" There was a mild reproach in his voice.

"I know you have and I know you mean to keep it, but I just have the strangest feeling." She shook her head. "Don't mind me. Maybe I'm just nervous."

"About what?"

"Meeting your parents. It's an intimidating thought."

"It shouldn't be. I've already told you they'll adore you. They'd love anyone who'd take me on at this stage and promise to produce lots of grandchildren. They've been waiting for that ever since my twenty-first birthday, I think."

Stacy's heart felt as though it had somersaulted inside her chest. "Grandchildren?" she repeated in a whisper.

"Sure. Isn't that what this is all about?"

"Explain yourself, Congressman. You're not making yourself very clear."

He gave her an exasperated look. "You haven't gone suddenly daft on me, have you? I thought we'd been discussing marriage all along. At least that's what I've been discussing. Did you have another arrangement in mind?"

"I . . . I didn't have any arrangement at all in mind," Stacy said slowly. "I mean . . . you never said the words before."

He gave her a taunting grin. "I had no idea you were expecting a formal proposal, Miss Allen. But, if that's what it takes, let's get on with it."

He pulled the car to the side of the road, jumped out and bounded around to her side. Yanking open her door with a flourish, he ordered, "Out. Right now."

Stacy looked at him as though he'd gone suddenly mad.

"What now?"

"You wanted a proposal and you shall have one," he said, falling to one knee in front of her.

Taking her hand in his, he intoned solemnly, "Miss Allen, if you would do me the great honor of becoming my wife, I promise to love, honor, and cherish you all the rest of our days."

He looked so absurd, kneeling there in the dirt that was still damp from the morning rain that Stacy felt an urge to giggle. Instead, her voice catching in her throat, she said, "Congressman, I'd be honored to marry you."

"Wait," he cautioned. "You haven't heard it all."

"There's more?"

"Absolutely. You have to promise to love, honor, and obey me."

Stacy shook her head in mock sorrow. "I knew there had to be a catch to it."

"Catch? What catch? It seems only fair that you promise to obey me. And if I don't get that commitment from you now, I'll be lost after we're married. You'll be snooping around the halls of Congress looking for exposés to put on the air and before I know it, I'll be out of office."

"Haven't you learned anything by now?" Stacy asked, her voice severe. "If we were married, I couldn't possibly investigate your activities. Besides, you've told me repeatedly you have nothing to hide."

He appeared to consider her remarks, then nodded as though he was satisfied with the reply.

"That's true," he said. "In that case, then, I guess I'll marry you whether you agree to obey me or not."

"Thank goodness," Stacy said, with a dramatic sigh of relief. "For a minute there I thought you were trying to back out."

"Never," he said, his voice suddenly serious. Pulling her down with him, they lay sprawled in the dirt and grass. He kissed her with a lingering passion that slowly built toward a crescendo. Stacy trembled in his arms.

Then, in a sudden burst of energy, he was standing, brushing himself off.

"Okay. That's settled," he said in a calm, business-like voice. "Let's get going."

Stacy peered up at him from where she remained on the ground. "That's it?" she asked.

He reached down and scooped her into his arms and gave her a quick, brotherly peck on the cheek.

"It will have to be . . . for now. My parents are going to have enough difficulty understanding why we're arriving on their doorstep looking as though we've been rolling around in a haystack without us being an hour late besides."

"Good Lord," Stacy said, looking down in horror at her rumpled blouse and beige slacks, which were streaked with dirt and blades of grass. "Wayne, I can't meet your parents looking like this. Couldn't we stop by the hotel long enough for me to change? You can call from there and let them know we're on our way."

He surveyed her from top to toe and then nodded. "You're right. They'd never accept a daughter-in-law who walked in looking like you do. They'll think you're a wanton woman."

Stacy laughed. "I'm not that bad, but I do think it would be nice to make a decent first impression."

"Okay," he agreed. "But make it fast. I still have a plane to catch in a few hours."

At the hotel Stacy found her box crammed full with messages, most of them from the friends she'd planned to see over the weekend. There were also at least five from Jay.

"I wonder what he wants now?" she muttered under her breath as she rode the elevator up to her room. Whatever it was, it could wait until she'd returned from her evening with Wayne's parents.

During the brief drive from the hotel to Beverly Hills, Stacy managed to put the ominous pile of messages from Jay out of her mind. She observed the passing scenery with wonder, recalling how she'd felt on her first drive through the wealthy neighborhood a few years earlier. She'd been impressed by the perfectly manicured lawns, the profusion of colorful plants, and the elegant homes that seemed so small from the street. Once inside, however, Stacy discovered the smallness was an illusion. The estates had huge backyards, often with pools and tennis courts, as well as small guest houses. She wondered if the Dodges' home would be like that.

As Wayne pulled into the driveway of a white brick house with a circular driveway, the front door flew open and an older version of Wayne stepped out. The tall, trim man had the same athletic build, the same twinkling eyes and the same unruly hair, although his was more silver than dark now.

"Son," he greeted Wayne enthusiastically, embracing him. "How are you? And you must be the young lady we've been hearing so much about. Stacy, isn't it?"

"How do you do, Mr. Dodge?" Stacy returned his smile. "I'm so glad to meet you. I can see now why Wayne's so handsome."

"You've found a real charmer, boy. You hang onto her."

Wayne grinned. "I intend to."

"Well, let's not just stand around out here all evening. Come on in and meet Mrs. Dodge. She's been fluttering around here for the last four hours to make sure everything is just so."

As they entered the foyer, a smartly dressed older woman came in and overheard the remark. "Sam Dodge, you make me sound like a giddy old fool."

"You're anything but that, mother," Wayne said. He kissed her soundly on the cheek.

"Your father doesn't seem to think so," she said huffily, though she gave her husband a broad wink as she spoke.

"Come on, Marjorie, admit it," he teased. "You've been a wreck ever since Wayne called and said he was bringing Stacy home. You've been running every which way."

"Well, you were no help. Honestly, Wayne, your father would welcome the Queen of England in his bathrobe and have her sit down to tea at the kitchen table," she chided him fondly.

"The Queen would probably find it a refreshing change," he retorted. "Besides, Stacy is not the Queen of England. She's practically a member of the family. Right, my dear?"

Stacy blushed. "I hope so."

"What do you mean you hope so?" Wayne asked indignantly. "You've already said yes. You can't change your mind now."

"She's said she'll marry you?" Mrs. Dodge asked excitedly, looking from one to the other. "That's wonderful!"

She gave Stacy a warm hug.

"I can't tell you how thrilled I am. This son of mine has been a bachelor for far too long. I was sure no woman would ever want him now that he's so set in his ways. These Dodge men are stubborn enough when they're young. They get even worse as they get older."

"Now, mother, don't you try to frighten Stacy," Wayne said.

Stacy grinned. "I know exactly what you mean, Mrs. Dodge. Perhaps, I should reconsider after all."

"Now look what you've done, Marjorie," Mr. Dodge said with mock severity. "Let's get these young people a drink and toast their engagement before you say something else to get them to break it."

That teasing exchange had set the tone for the rest of the evening. The older couple was so excited about the prospect of Wayne marrying at last and, as he had predicted, providing them with grandchildren, that they could talk of little else.

As they were leaving, Mrs. Dodge hugged Stacy.

"You come back here and see us before you leave Los Angeles, my dear. From now on this is your home and you're welcome here anytime."

"Thank you, Mrs. Dodge. You're a very special family. I'm glad I'm going to be a part of it."

When they were on their way back to the hotel, Wayne said, "Well, you certainly were a big hit. Didn't I tell you not to worry?"

"Your parents are wonderful."

"Frankly, I have a feeling they're going to be fonder of you than they are of me."

Stacy looked at him and grinned. "Don't tell me you're jealous."

"Maybe I am," he admitted, with a rueful smile. "Sometimes after my father and I get into one of our long, angry debates, they don't invite me back for weeks. You've already been given a standing invitation."

"That's because I didn't discuss politics with them," Stacy reminded him. "Can you imagine how your father would feel if I told him my position on most issues was remarkably similar to yours. He'd probably demand custody of our children."

"Probably," Wayne agreed with a laugh. "Keep that in mind after the children are born."

"I'll try to remember," Stacy promised.

At the hotel, they walked through the lobby together. Stacy wasn't concerned about being seen with Wayne. Her professional objectivity was far from her mind. Upstairs, they stopped in front of her door and Wayne kissed her lightly.

"I don't think I'd better come in. I might not want to leave."

"I might not want you to," Stacy whispered, her hand resting on his chest as she gazed up into his eyes.

"Are you actually suggesting that I stay?" he asked hopefully, pulling her tightly against him.

"No," she said quickly, adding at his look of

disappointment, "Sorry, Congressman. Maybe your luck will improve, when I get back to Washington."

"Promises, promises," he said, with a resigned sigh. "You'd better watch that, Miss Allen, or you'll end up with more than you bargained for one of these days."

"I doubt it, Congressman. I think I know exactly what I'm getting," she said softly, her words muffled as he held her close to him, his hands stroking her back.

"I'll miss you," he murmured against her ear, his teeth nipping playfully.

"I'll be back in a couple of days."

"A lot can happen in a couple of days," he reminded her. "Just look at how things have changed in the last two."

The sound of the elevator doors opening down the hall forced them apart, but not before Wayne had given her one last kiss, a demanding meeting of their lips that took her breath away. Then he was gone, striding purposefully away without another word.

Stacy stood watching him with a mixture of regret at being left behind and joy at the prospect of what lay ahead for them. She could hardly wait to return to Washington, end her work on this documentary and then shout to the whole world that she and Wayne had fallen in love. As she stood there day-dreaming, she heard the insistent ringing of the phone in her room. Fumbling frantically for her key, she managed at last to unlock the door, switch on a light and grab for the phone.

"Hello," she answered breathlessly.

"Stacy, where the devil have you been?"

"Hi, Jay," she said, calmly ignoring his demanding tone.

"I asked you where you've been," he repeated

sharply. "I've been calling all weekend. Didn't you get my messages?"

Stacy was growing tired of his attitude. "I've got a whole handful of messages, Jay," she said impatiently. "I haven't had time to return any of them yet. I got to the hotel later than I'd planned."

"I thought you were due in Friday night. They said at the front desk that you had checked in."

"Who made you my keeper? Look, not that it's any of your business, but I spent most of the weekend with friends," she said stretching the truth slightly. "Now what do you want?"

"I want you to come downstairs and meet me in the coffee shop. There's someone here you should meet."

"Are you out of your mind, Jay? I'm exhausted. It's late. I'm in no mood to meet anyone at this hour."

"Stacy, it's important. I promise you won't be tired after you hear this."

"Jay, what are you up to now?" Stacy asked wearily. "Is this important to you or to me?"

"Both of us actually unless I'm wrong about the sort of reporter you are."

She knew he wouldn't give up until she'd agreed to come downstairs. She might as well get it over with.

"Okay," she said reluctantly. "I'll be there in a few minutes."

Suddenly that same nameless sense of dread that had assailed Stacy earlier in the evening came back, exerting its full force. As she put pens and a notebook into her purse, she tried to fight off the feeling of foreboding that seemed centered at the pit of her stomach. But no matter how much she argued with herself, she faced the prospect of meeting Jay and his mysterious companion with increasing anxiety.

When she entered the coffee shop on the hotel's lower level, she spotted Jay at once. He was seated in a corner booth with a Mexican woman, who appeared to be in her mid-forties, and two young girls. As Stacy neared their table, she realized with a sense of shock that the woman was much younger than she had appeared at a distance. She couldn't be more than twenty-five or so. Her prematurely gray hair and worried expression made her look older.

Jay was on his feet as soon as he saw her.

"Here you are. Stacy, I'd like you to meet Maria Lopez and her daughters, Miranda and Carmen."

"How do you do?" Stacy said politely, giving Jay a puzzled glance.

The woman stared at her from dark, frightened eyes, but the two girls smiled shyly, their brown eyes seeming huge in their tiny, nut-brown faces.

Stacy slid into the booth next to Jay and whispered, "What's this all about?"

"Patience, love," he told her, obviously enjoying her confusion. To Maria he said in a kind, low voice, "Tell Miss Allen about your job, Maria."

In a halting mix of Spanish and English, the woman began to talk about the work she and her older daughters did for a company that manufactured dresses. They worked at home and were paid by the piece, earning only a few cents for each completed garment.

Stacy looked at her in disbelief. That was far below minimum wage for even one person, much less for the three of them.

"That's illegal, Maria. You are entitled to earn much more than that. The law protects you. Why do you do it?"

Maria's eyes filled with fear at the probing question. She turned to Jay for support.

"It's okay, Maria. You can tell her the truth. Stacy won't get you into any trouble."

"You are sure?" she asked hesitantly, her voice soft and tremulous. Jay nodded.

"I not here legally," she told Stacy. "The hombre . . . the man say if I don't take money he give me and stay quiet, he send me back to Mexico."

Her eyes took on a stubborn glow and there was a determined set to her face, when she said forcefully, "We never go back. Never." Her head shook vehemently to emphasize her declaration.

Jay patted her hand, while he explained to Stacy, "Her family was very poor. When her husband died, they couldn't afford to support her and her children. She and the girls—there are two more at home— came here to try to start over."

Stacy's face reflected the horror she felt at the plight of this desperate family.

"But, wait," Jay said, "there's more. Maria, tell Miss Allen the name of the company you work for."

Stacy shrugged at the mention of the name. "I never heard of it."

"I really didn't think you would have," Jay said, pausing before delivering his most shocking piece of information. "But if you check it out, Stacy, you'll find that one of the principal stockholders is Wayne Dodge."

Stacy's mouth dropped open in disbelief, as a cold feeling of panic took her in its grip. "No," she whispered.

"Yes, Stacy."

She tried to make her voice firm. "You've . . . you've got to be wrong, Jay. Wayne couldn't . . . he wouldn't be involved in something like this. He's too decent and kind. He'd be just as shocked about what's happening to Maria as we are."

Jay took her hand. "I know you don't want to

believe it, Stacy, but it's true. There's no doubt in my mind. I've checked the incorporation papers myself."

Stacy looked from Jay to the woman seated across the table. Maria's hands, roughened by work, twisted nervously, as she watched Stacy. Then Stacy looked at the two children in their neatly pressed dresses that were frayed and far too small. Her eyes filled with tears of rage and shame, rage that something like this could happen to these poor, desperate people and shame that she had fallen in love with the man who was apparently responsible.

"Jay, let me out of here," she demanded, her voice a despairing cry. He moved aside and let her go without comment.

Running blindly from the coffee shop, she raced to the elevator and punched repeatedly at the button, as if it would heed her urgent command and arrive more swiftly. Inside at last, she leaned weakly against the side as it rose rapidly to her floor. With each passing floor, she found herself fighting to maintain her last shred of control.

In her room she pounded on the bed in futile anger, her tears flowing freely now. Over and over she repeated that Jay had to be wrong. He had to be. But she knew he would never have come to her at all, unless he had checked his information thoroughly. As badly as he wanted to beat Wayne in the next election, Jay would never stoop to vicious mudslinging without being very sure of himself. It was not his style.

Eleven

It was the longest night of Stacy's life. She lay in
bed watching the seconds tick by on the illuminated
dial of her travel alarm clock, waiting for the first
streaks of daybreak to brighten the sky. The wait
seemed interminable.

With each passing second she examinied the hours
she had spent with Wayne over the last few weeks,
turning each moment over in her mind like a geo-
metric puzzle that must be examined from all sides
to be understood.

Moaning softly with an unbearable anguish, she
pounded her fist into the pillow.

"No! No! No!" she whispered softly. "I won't believe
it."

And yet, she had to admit that the evidence was
damning. In the morning she could set out to discover the truth for herself, but until then she could
only live with her doubts and cling to the slim hope
that it had all been some horrible misunderstanding.

It was almost a relief when the hands of the clock
reached 6:00 A.M. She crawled from the bed and

pulled on her bright green warm-up suit, her running shoes and a headband. Then she slipped through the hotel's silent hallways to the street.

A morning shroud of fog hung over the city, obscuring the mountains to the east. The air was cool and damp, really perfect for jogging, but Stacy was oblivious to the weather, to everything but the painful task ahead of her. She tried to concentrate on her breathing. Inhale deeply. Exhale slowly. Another deep breath. Her skin grew damp from the exertion and her heart pounded. Her body was beginning to feel alive and refreshed, despite the lack of sleep, but her mind refused to give up the search for answers.

Back in her room, her message light was on.

"Who on earth would be calling at this hour?" she wondered aloud, as she dialed the front desk.

"Yes, Miss Allen?"

"You have a message for me?"

"Just a minute and I'll check." There was a brief pause and then, "You have two messages. Your office called and would like you to call back immediately and a Congressman Dodge called. He said he'd try again later."

A few hours ago the early morning call from Wayne would have made her heart sing, but now the message rang bitterly in her ears. Fighting back tears, she returned Pete's call.

"Della, it's Stacy. Pete wanted to talk to me."

"Hi, Stacy. I'll put him right on."

When Pete finally spoke, there was a harsh, unyielding tone to his voice that Stacy recognized immediately. He was furious.

"Stacy, I want you on the next flight home."

"But, Pete—"

"No arguments. If you want to salvage your job, young lady, you'll get back here in record time. You have some explaining to do."

"I don't understand."

"Neither do I. That's why I want you back here."

"Pete, I haven't even started yet," she argued, though she could tell from Pete's attitude that there was little point to prolonging the discussion.

"Leave your notes for Don Sampson. He'll be out there by noon today and he can pick them up at the hotel desk."

"But, Pete, I want to finish this story. You're the one who insisted I do it, remember? Please. You've got to let me check out some information before I come back."

There was a sigh on Pete's end of the line.

"Stacy, you're not listening to me. You are off of the Wayne Dodge documentary as of this instant and if you are not in my office within twenty-four hours you are also out of a job. Am I making myself clear enough for you now?"

"I'll be back," she said, biting off each word, as she tried to restrain her own mounting fury. With that she slammed down the receiver.

Sitting on the edge of the bed, she held her head in her hands. What on earth was happening? The whole world seemed to have suddenly gone mad. At least her world had. Pete's refusal to explain his autocratic order to come home made no sense. Nor, for that matter, did his insistence that she return now. And how was she going to discover the truth about Wayne and this horrible company, if she went back to Washington without checking the records herself? She certainly wasn't going to turn that piece of information over to Don Sampson. She couldn't. If it were true, it could destroy Wayne.

The realization that she loved Wayne too deeply to see him publicly crucified, no matter his guilt or innocence, shook Stacy almost as deeply as Jay's original revelation the previous night. Although Pete couldn't possibly know the depth of her love for

Wayne, he had been right to remove her from the documentary. She had lost her objectivity. She was no longer thinking as a reporter, but as a woman in love. She wanted to find the truth, not for her viewers, but to prove to herself that Wayne hadn't lied to her.

Slowly, she dialed the airlines and checked on return flights to Washington. There was one leaving in ninety minutes. With any luck at all, she could be on it. If she made it, it would be the first lucky break she'd had in the last few hours of turmoil.

Two hours later, angry, hurt and confused, Stacy was on her way back home. Cup after cup of coffee, strong and black, were making her even more jittery than she had been. She fought an almost irresistible urge to move to the smoking section of the plane and ask someone for a cigarette. She had given up her short-lived habit two years earlier and she wasn't going to allow this problem to ruin her record of abstinence.

Finally, unable to rest or to focus on her book, she pulled a stack of papers from her briefcase and began studying them. They were the copies of incorporation papers and other reports on the Ray-Tech Garment Company, the firm Jay claimed Wayne had founded with several other backers a decade ago. It was the same company which allegedly paid outrageously low wages to Maria Lopez and her daughters. As Stacy went over and over the material, she began formulating a plan, a way to determine once and for all whether Wayne was in fact involved in the exploitation of illegal immigrants.

She was so thoroughly engrossed in making notes that, by the time the flight landed in Washington, she had driven all thought of Pete's anger from her mind. Instead of dreading the upcoming encounter with him, she was merely anxious to get to the station and begin following through on her plan.

She picked up her luggage, caught a cab home and transferred everything to her own car in record time. She headed toward the station without even going upstairs to her apartment.

At the office Stacy went straight to her desk, dropped off her briefcase and looked around the room for the reporter who covered business and economic news. Walt Dixon had been on the beat for years and if anyone could help her get to the bottom of this, he could. She finally spotted him standing over a wire machine, his fat cigar clamped between his teeth. She went over to wait for him at his desk.

"How ya doin', Stacy?" he asked, dumping the yards and yards of wire copy on top of his desk, which was already littered with empty paper cups and cigar butts. "You need something?"

"Walt, I need your help. I want everything you can find out about a California firm called the Ray-Tech Garment Company."

"Anything in particular you're looking for?"

"The company's reputation, its business practices, any dirt you can come up with," she said, then added as casually as she could manage, "and I'd like to know who's running it, any big stockholders, that sort of thing. Can you do it?"

"Sure. When do you need it?"

"As soon as possible."

"Okay, kid, I'll do my best. You gonna be around awhile?"

"I'll be at my desk."

"No," said a voice just behind her. "You'll be in my office."

Stacy turned to find Pete looming over her, a scowl on his face. Suddenly she recalled his demand that she see him at once following her return.

"Pete, I'm sorry. I wanted to check on something before seeing you."

"Just get into my office," he ordered gruffly.

Meekly, Stacy followed him across the newsroom, aware that several other reporters were eyeing them with unhidden curiosity. Once they were inside Pete's office with the door shut, she sat nervously on the edge of a chair.

"Okay, Pete. What's this all about?"

"This," he said, tossing the Style section of the *Washington Post* over to her. "Take a look at the Ear column and see what the local gossips are talking about today all over town."

Stacy's eyes skimmed the page looking for the popular column. When she found it, Wayne's name seemed to jump out at her, followed by her own.

"Oh my God," she whispered, looking up at Pete. "I . . . I had no idea."

"Had no idea?" Pete exploded. "How the hell could you not have known about this? Engagements don't make the front of the *Post*'s Style section unless someone announces them."

"We didn't announce anything," Stacy insisted.

"But you don't deny that you are engaged to Wayne Dodge?"

"I'm not . . . I'm not sure anymore."

"What do you mean you're not sure? Are you or aren't you?"

Stacy's eyes suddenly filled with the tears she'd been unable to shed all through the night and this dreadful, long day.

"Pete, I don't know. Can't we just leave it at that for now," she begged.

"No," he said adamantly. "Good Lord, Stacy, don't you realize how much trouble you're in? I begged you to tell me if you were having a relationship with Wayne Dodge. You denied it and I kept you on the documentary. Now I read in the *Washington Post* that you and the Congressman have just spent a romantic little weekend at Malibu and that you're about to announce your engagement. I'm trying very hard not to fire you, but if you won't explain all of this to me and explain it fast, I'll have no choice."

"I can't explain it," she said stubbornly. "Not now."

"Then you're relieved of duty," Pete said wearily. "I'm sorry, Stacy."

"Yeah, Pete," Stacy said slowly. "So am I."

Shaking, she got to her feet and started out of the office, still unable to absorb the fact that her career at this station was over. At the door she paused and looked back at Pete, but he couldn't seem to face her. It was probably just as well, she thought with a sigh as she went back to her desk to gather up her briefcase and the few personal belongings in her desk.

As though she were controlled by some force outside of herself, Stacy managed to make the drive home. In her apartment she sank down on the sofa and stared blindly into the darkness. Suddenly it all came crashing down around her. The job she had wanted so much was over. The man she loved might merely have been using her. Where could she go? What could she do to make this pain inside her go away?

The doorbell rang, shattering the silence. It took several moments for Stacy to orient herself in the darkness. Fumbling for the light switch, she turned on a soft lamp whose glow was just bright enough to allow her to make her way to the door.

"Who's there?"

"Wayne."

Numbly she opened the door and stared at him.

"Honey, what's wrong?" he asked, his expression instantly filled with concern. "What's happened? You look terrible."

"Thanks a lot," she said, returning to her place on

the sofa without waiting to see if he followed her inside. "How did you know I was home?"

"I called the hotel and found out you'd checked out this morning. I called the station then and Della told me you were on your way home. Honey, please, tell me what's happened."

Stacy looked up at him, drinking in the sight of his tall, lean body. At the thought of the moments she had spent in his arms, she trembled with a desire it was almost impossible for her to ignore. How could she still want him so much? And yet she did, in spite of everything.

He sat next to her, but made no attempt to touch her, as though sensing that something had changed in their relationship. Instinctively he understood the need for caution and she was grateful to him for that. Finally, in a small, weak voice, she spoke.

"I've lost my job," she said, trying to sound as though it didn't matter.

"What?" he said, his tone shocked. "When? Why?"

Suddenly Stacy had an uncontrollable urge to giggle. Rapidly the giggles turned into a kind of hysteria, bordering between laughter and tears. "You . . . you sound like a . . . a reporter," she said brokenly. "Who? What? When? Where?"

"Stacy," he said, gathering her into his arms and crushing her to him. "Sweetheart, please talk to me about it. Tell me what's happened."

She shook her head. "I can't," she managed between sobs.

For several minutes he held her tightly and at last she felt as if some of his strength was seeping into her. He pulled a handkerchief from his pocket and wiped away the dampness on her cheeks.

"It was because of the story in the paper. Didn't you see it?" she asked, when she could speak.

"I saw it," he said flatly. "But why would you lose

your job over that. It was nothing but a gossip column."

"Gossip," Stacy said, jerking herself from his arms. "Is that all it was? Gossip?"

He saw the fury flashing in her eyes.

"Stacy, all I meant was that it's certainly not the sort of thing people lose their jobs over."

"In my business it is. Wayne, I've told you all along that it was wrong for me to be seeing you. I thought I could get through this documentary and then it wouldn't matter anymore. How was I supposed to know that someone in California would leap at the chance to tell the world what we did out there?"

"Stacy, we didn't *do* anything out there," Wayne said impatiently.

"We were together. That was all Pete needed to know."

"I'll talk to him."

"No you won't," she said defiantly. "Stay out of it."

Wayne began pacing up and down in front of her. "All right, then, you tell me what you want me to do. If you don't want me to talk to Pete, isn't there something else I can do? I have friends at other stations."

"Forget it," she snapped. "I'll find my own jobs, thank you."

He looked at her sharply, startled by her tone.

"Stacy, there's more to this than you're telling me. What else is wrong?"

Before she could answer, the doorbell rang again.

"Who are you expecting?" Wayne demanded.

"No one," she said, going to the door. "Who is it?"

"It's Walt Dixon, Stacy."

Stacy threw open the door. "Walt, what are you doing here?"

The reporter looked behind her at Wayne Dodge,

whose expression was far from welcoming. "Is this a bad time?" he asked.

"No, of course not," she said. "Please come in. It's just that I wasn't expecting you."

"I found the information you wanted. I went over to your desk and someone told me what had happened, that Pete had sent you home. I thought this might be important to you anyway, so I decided I'd bring it on over."

"I doubt I'll be needing it now, but thanks anyway, Walt. I appreciate your bringing it by."

"Sure, kid. I still hope it helps. I don't know what you were looking for, but it appears you may have been onto something. That Ray-Tech outfit has a long string of complaints against it."

At the mention of Ray-Tech, Stacy turned to look at Wayne, noticing that he seemed to turn pale beneath his tan and that his mouth tightened. At his sides his hands were clenching and unclenching. The sudden tension in his stance, his expression, everything about him pointed to guilt. She turned back to Walt, who was watching them both with interest.

When Stacy faced him, he said quickly, "Look, kid, I just wanted to drop this off. I'd better be going."

"Thanks, Walt."

"Sure. I hope things work out for you."

Then he was gone and Stacy and Wayne were alone again. They faced each other like wary opponents, neither of them speaking. At last he broke the silence.

"What did you want to know about Ray-Tech?"

"You've heard of it then?" Stacy replied, ignoring his question.

"I've heard of it," he said flatly. "It's up to its corporate neck in illegal aliens. It would be impossible to find a dirtier operation. How did you hear about it? Our investigation hasn't been released yet."

"Your investigation?" Stacy repeated blankly.

He studied her closely for several minutes, then said abruptly, "Sit down."

When Stacy was seated on the sofa, he sat next to her.

"What I am about to tell you is off the record, okay? If this information gets out now, it could blow months of work. Do I have your word?"

She nodded.

"All right. You know we've been trying to crack down on the businesses in Southern California that encourage illegal immigrants to come into this country to work and then exploit them. To do that we needed to find out who was behind the operation. We figured there had to be a couple of guys at the top controlling things, the same way there is in drug smuggling.

"A few years ago I had loaned some money to an old friend to help him get started in the garment business. In return he insisted I become a major stockholder."

"Ray-Tech," Stacy whispered in sudden understanding.

"Exactly. The owner is a man named Marty Farrell. He agreed to work with us and let us use Ray-Tech to try to find the answers we needed. For months now he's been hiring the aliens trying to win the confidence of the key men in the operation. In another couple of weeks we should have all the evidence we need to shut down the biggest illegal alien smuggling operation in the Southwest."

Stacy thought of Maria Lopez and the others who had been so badly abused and cheered for what Wayne and the others were doing. Then she realized what it all meant and a smile lit up her face.

Her relief was so great that she threw her arms around Wayne's neck and kissed him soundly. As their lips met, it was as though the last twenty-four hours had never happened and they were back in their own private world on the beach at Malibu. When they separated, breathless after their heated embrace, Wayne's eyes were sparkling with a devilish, predatory gleam.

"My goodness," he whispered huskily against her neck. "If I'd had any idea of the response I'd get, I would have told you about the investigation days ago."

Stacy's laugh quickly turned to a soft moan, as his lips found the sensitive, bare skin at the deep V of her blouse. His mouth, warm and moist against her flesh, traveled slowly and sensuously along her neck, her cheeks until, at last, it reached her own lips, parted to receive the kiss. Her fingers were curled into the thickness of his hair at the back of his neck and she could feel the tremor that shook him as their tongues met.

Slowly he pulled back, his breathing ragged, but his eyes revealing a determination to regain some measure of self-control.

"We have some more talking to do," he said, as his hands idly massaged the side of her neck.

"We won't have much of a conversation, if you keep that up," she teased lightly, capturing his hand in her own.

"Fair enough," he said, smiling into her eyes. "Now, then, tell me why you were so interested in Ray-Tech."

"Wouldn't you rather do this some more?" she asked, kissing him quickly.

"Absolutely, you shameless little temptress. But we'll have no more of that until you've given me some answers," he insisted sternly.

"Okay. Okay," she agreed reluctantly. Searching

for a way to begin, she finally said, "I met a woman who works for Ray-Tech. She's one of the aliens who's being exploited. I was horrified at what she told me and I was trying to find out more about the company."

"And?" he asked expectantly.

"And what?"

"Stacy, there has to be more or you wouldn't have looked at me the way you did a little while ago, when that man mentioned the company."

"I . . . I had seen your name on the incorporation papers," she said slowly, exhaling a sigh of relief that it was all in the open at last.

"I guess I just don't understand you at all," Wayne said. "You claim you love me and yet you apparently believed I was capable of operating a company that exploits human misery."

"I didn't believe it."

"Stacy, there's no point in your trying to deny it. You were checking it out."

"Don't you see," she pleaded. "I had to. The papers were right there in front of me. I couldn't just ignore them. I had to prove they were a lie."

"But they weren't. I do own a large part of that company."

"Yes, but you're not hiring illegal aliens to exploit them."

"Oh, but I am. You have only my word that there's an investigation going on. I could be lying to you."

Stacy fought against the cold fear that seemed to wash over her. Then she shook her head.

"No. You're not lying to me. I'd stake my life on it. You're not capable of any of those things. The man who wrote that speech I read at Malibu couldn't do those things."

"Are you sure?" he asked.

"I'm sure," she said with certainty.

"But you do see how the truth may not always be what it seems?" he asked, forcing her to examine her instincts as a reporter.

Wayne was right. If she ever again worked as a journalist, she would have to learn to dig beneath the surface truth. Twice now in the weeks she had known him she had come close to indicting him on circumstantial evidence. No one would have questioned her interpretation of the information she had and yet any reporting of the facts as she had first seen them would have been a twisted version of the truth.

"Okay, Congressman, you've made your point."

"Then there's one other point I'd like to make tonight."

Stacy felt the fear rising inside her again. "What's that?"

"This," he said, his lips grinding against hers in a demanding search for submission. She gave in to the demand weakly, her pulse beginning to race as she felt herself drawn against the solid hardness of his muscled body.

"I love you," he mumbled hoarsely as his lips left hers for barely a fraction of a second before claiming them again in another bruising kiss. His hands were equally insistent, as they began a thorough exploration of her body. His fingers brought the sensitive tips of her breasts to a throbbing fullness that strained against the lacy material of her bra. Then those same gentle, persuasive hands roamed downward over the rest of her body, lifting her blouse to stroke her bared midriff, then continuing down to begin a slow massage of her thighs.

A warm glow was spreading through her body and she shivered in delicious spasms. Stacy gave herself up totally to the sensations being aroused by Wayne's expert stroking. When she began unbuttoning his shirt to allow her hands to feel the springy roughness of his chest with its mat of dark hair, he groaned and pulled her more tightly against him. Molded to fit the hard contours of his body, Stacy felt herself arching involuntarily toward him to heighten the tantalizing contact between them.

Then suddenly she felt herself being lifted off of the sofa by his strong arms.

"Where's the bedroom in this place?" he demanded gruffly, his breath a teasing tickle against her neck.

She tilted her head. "Through there," she murmured softly, a shy smile playing about her lips as she clung tightly to him. "Why are we going in there?"

"Don't be coy. You know damn good and well why we're going in there," he retorted, still breathless from their passion.

"You mean so we won't fall off the sofa," she asked with feigned innocence.

"Exactly," he said, laughing at last, as he dumped her unceremoniously onto the bed before falling down beside her.

She curled herself into his body and whispered provocatively into his ear, "But I thought we were going to wait."

His eyes met hers, noting that they were filled with a passion that matched his own. "Is that what you want?" he asked seriously.

"No," she said, her lips seeking his. "No, my love."

Then they were lost to a gathering momentum of sensations, lifting them higher and higher to a peak of excitement that was totally new to Stacy. Gasping in joy, she clung to Wayne as their perfectly attuned bodies reached the edge of a precipice and ecstatically tumbled over together.

At last, as they lay in each other's arms, their breathing returned to normal.

"Tell me something," Stacy requested, her eyes bright and dancing with barely suppressed laughter.

"Anything," Wayne agreed.

"Does this mean I get first crack at the story on the investigation?"

"It does not," he said, giving her a playful smack.

"But that's not fair."

"Who ever told you life was fair, my sweet?" he teased.

"Please," she begged, trailing a row of kisses along his bare chest.

"My God, woman, you don't play fair," he said, his breath beginning once more to come in ragged gasps.

"Who ever told you life was fair?" she mocked.

"Okay. Okay. You win," he said, groaning under the onslaught of her kisses. "As long as this is my reward, I think I'd give you almost anything you wanted."

"Almost anything?" she asked, nipping at his ear.

"You don't give up, do you? All right, anything," he agreed, rolling her over and pinning her down, as his lips sought hers.

"Know something, Congressman?" she asked, when she could speak again.

"Now what?" he asked resignedly.

"I think we make one heck of a team."

"Oh? Are we going out for sports?" he inquired curiously.

"Hardly. I was thinking more in terms of marriage."

"You were, were you?"

"Weren't you?" Stacy asked, her voice tremulous and her eyes wide with a sudden feeling of panic. Wasn't that what this was all about?

Wayne's booming laughter filled the room.

"Don't look so horrified, Miss Allen. I've every intention of making an honest woman of you," he said lightly. "In fact, you couldn't get away from me now, if you tried."

His lips, branding hers with a hot possessiveness, sealed the bargain.